Throw Away Sisters
By
Debbie Winnekins Deutsch

Dw Deutsch

Throw Away Sisters

By Debbie Winnekins Deutsch

Copyrighted © Debbie Winnekins Deutsch 2016

All rights reserved.

ISBN-13: 978-1530730704
ISBN-10:1530730708

Cover Design: Ash Ahrens

Summary: Throw Away Sisters Is the compelling tale of fifteen-year-old Cart and her eleven-year-old sister, Lucy. When the grown-ups in their lives fail them, their options become stay, and contend with the dangers of abuse, or run away. They now face the most unacceptable outcome imaginable, the threat of separation. Throw Away Sisters is a tale of longing, sacrifice, and ultimately, hope.

Family is everything.

Debbie

Prologue

The first time I realized there were bad people in the world was several years ago when a local boy was abducted near his home. The police found him naked and dead a few days later at a campsite almost an hour away. I don't know why it hit me so hard. I didn't know him. I was little and didn't understand what had happened to him other than someone stole him from his mama and daddy. It scared me to know there were people who could hurt someone that way. I prayed no one like that would ever cross my path. Little did I know that Danny would show up. He is my mama's latest boyfriend. He doesn't seem like a pervert killer, but he makes me feel uneasy just the same. I shake my Magic 8 Ball and ask if Danny is a pervert killer. Taking a deep breath, I peek inside. **Better Not Tell You Now….**

1

My little sister Lucy and I sit quietly in the back of Danny's new, black 1978 Pontiac Firebird Trans Am. He strutted around like a rich guy when he bought it off the showroom floor. It's not quite the family car Mama imagined, but then Danny's not quite the family guy I imagined. I guess we both got a surprise. Mama always says, *"Cart, you have to take the good with the bad in life."* I've yet to see the good that's supposed to balance the bad. After three months of him hanging around, it's pretty obvious he will never be daddy material.

I'm not sure where Mama picked him up. She's singled out some class acts in the past, that's for sure. They must be attracted to her petite frame and big boobs. At least that's what I've overheard a time or two in conversations. I guess when you pair her body with thick, copper hair and piercing green eyes, you have a combination that is deadly to men. It terrifies me because I look like her, only my eyes are blue like my daddy's, and I don't have her boobs. Yet. Is that all guys are ever interested in?

My guess is Danny came about from a drunken, foggy night at a bar. Unfortunately, after Mama brought him home, he never left. Like the golden bird on the hood of his car, Danny is full of shit. How can I know he's all wrong, yet my mama thinks he's all right? And now because of Danny, we're on the move again.

In the past, Mama moved us around a lot so my daddy couldn't find us. We always stayed in Mason though. Daddy hasn't been around in so long, I forgot the last time I saw him. I miss him and love him. He's the only one who has ever really loved me and Lucy.

Now we're moving to another town. What fifteen-year-old girl wants to keep moving? I'd like to stay in one place long enough to make a friend or two. If we leave Mason, how will Daddy find us? Danny wants to move closer to his work. Mama begged him to take her with, pleading that she'd keep a good house and cook for him. I laughed out loud when I heard that. Mama shot me an evil look, willing me to keep my mouth shut. Keeping a good house and cooking are not in her vocabulary. I'm surprised she can say the words without choking on them. Anything domestic falls on me and Lucy. If Danny were even a tiny bit bright, he'd have figured that out by now.

And now we're in the car moving away from Mason. The open window blows my hair in all directions. I brush it out of my face and look down at my mood ring, sliding it around between my finger and thumb. The stone is a grayish color. Anxious, nervous and strained – that's me.

I gaze over at Lucy sitting next to me in the car. I can't believe she's going to be eleven in a couple of weeks. She talked me into letting her wear my favorite tie-dyed shirt and peace bracelet. The shirt fits her good for being four years younger than me. Her long, unruly blonde curls are braided into pigtails, which are flopping in the wind of the open car window.

Lucy reminds me a lot of our daddy. Mothering her has been my job from day one. I don't know where Mama's head is. I thought kids were supposed to be God's greatest creations, to be cherished and loved. Apparently, Mama never got the memo. I watch Lucy as she dozes off. Her head bobs and dips like one of those bobbleheaded dogs you see in the back window of a car. It makes me think back several years to my daddy and his Beatles bobblehead collection.

~

"Cart Baby, come check this out," Daddy calls to me.

I look up from my *Fun with Dick and Jane* book and smile. I feel proud being able to read from a book. I couldn't wait to learn how to do it. The only person I'd give up reading time for is my daddy. Laying the book down, I hurry over to him.

The show is about to begin. He lines up Paul, John, George and Ringo. With one hand, he moves the needle of the record player onto the record, and with the other hand, he goes down the line setting those heads to bobbing. Soon *Twist and Shout* comes pouring out.

I giggle, standing close to Daddy, as I watch those heads bobble to the beat of the music. I bobble my head too. I lean over and inhale the sweet cologne that mixes with the smell of my daddy and sigh. He catches me sniffing him again.

"Brut's a chick magnet, Cart," Daddy says, laughing. "Can't keep 'em off me with this stuff on."

I have no clue what he means but laugh anyway. Whenever my daddy laughs, I laugh. He musses up my hair and says, "Cart baby, you are the greatest. Did I ever tell you how you got your name?"

"Only a bazillion times," I answer, "but I want to hear it again."

Daddy sits down in the chair as the bobbleheads slow to a stop. I crawl up on his lap and snuggle in.

"Well, besides you and Lucy, you know I love everything about the Beatles, right?"

"Right," I say.

"Sometimes music speaks to your soul, you know, makes a difference in your life. Their music touches my heart, just

7

like you and your sister did on the day you were both born. It's a bitchin' feeling, you know?"

Daddy pauses and looks into my curious blue eyes. It looks as if his are tearing up a bit but then he shakes his head and continues.

"Your mama would not let me name you Beatle, for whatever reason."

Daddy rolls his eyes. I do, too, and giggle.

"And since you're a girl, Paul, John, George and Ringo didn't seem quite right. But then, I think McCartney – yeah, McCartney, that's a fine girl's name. I had friends who were naming their kids Rainbow, Peace and Freedom, so I should be able to call my sweet baby girl McCartney, right?"

"Right," I say.

"And so it was," Daddy says, hugging me. "My sweet little "Cart" McCartney Ann Matthews came to be."

I smile up at Daddy, squeezing him as tight as I can. Love swells over the top of my heart. Sometimes, I feel like my heart will burst. Even if Daddy is having a bad day, he always makes me feel loved. I lean back and look at Daddy's face. All of a sudden it looks sad.

"You don't know your Grandma, and that might not be a bad thing," Daddy adds. "She is a gruff old bird who couldn't show love or affection if it bit her square on the butt."

I remember Daddy talking about his mama once before. He never says much about her. I think she might live in a nearby town.

"Why is she so cranky?" I ask. "She should be happy, like you."

"She never told me what her deal is and won't talk about it. But I feel like somehow it's my fault," he says. "I never knew what love was until I met your mama. But now she's growing distant from me, thinks the grass is greener on the other side."

Daddy pauses. I can see the sadness in the lines on his face. I'm not sure what he's talking about, but I do know I want to erase the frown on his mouth. He looks at me and smiles.

"But it hasn't been all bad because you came along and four years later came Lucy. No family is perfect. My family, well, my mama, has a whole list of issues and your mama's family..." he begins to say and then pauses, with a twinkle in his eye.

We both smile, and at the same time, because I've heard it so many times before, say, "And Mama's family is nothing but two-bit trailer trash who'd throw you to the wolves to save themselves."

Daddy and I laugh and snort, even though I'm not quite sure what it means. It wasn't until later on that I'd learn the meaning of that phrase far too well.

"Now, don't you tell your mama," Daddy says, trying to be serious. "She'd hang us both out on the line to dry for thinking like that about her family."

"It'll be our secret, Daddy," I say, hugging him tight.

Over time, Mama and Daddy grew further apart. It was 1969 when Daddy left us and went to the Vietnam War. I didn't understand any of it.

"Daddy, please don't go." I cry and cry, the day he leaves. "I promise I'll be good and help take care of Lucy. Please stay. Please."

I throw myself against him and cry as hard as I ever have. Mama stands in the doorway holding Lucy, her green eyes expressionless. Then, she turns and shuts the door. Daddy sees Mama go back into the house. He looks so sad. He scoops me up and squeezes me.

"Oh, my sweet little McCartney," he says soothingly. He strokes my hair. "I'm not leaving because you're bad. I need to get some discipline, become a better person. I need to make your mama proud. I promise you I will come back."

And he eventually did come back, almost a year later. I don't know what a dishonorable discharge is and I don't care. I got my daddy back. Or so I thought. I soon discovered the daddy that came home was different from the daddy that left. Mama said he saw ugly things in Vietnam that he refused to talk about. I was only seven by then, but could tell something was off. I knew he still loved me and Lucy like he always had, but he'd lost that sparkle in his eyes. He and Mama drifted apart even more. They fought a lot, and Mama moved us a lot, but Daddy always found us. I took great comfort in that.

"June, they're my damn kids, you can't run off with them whenever you feel like it," he'd yell through the locked door, after finding us once again.

"Go away, Jack," Mama would yell back. "Get off the drugs and booze and knock on my door when you're sober. Then we'll talk."

"How the hell can we talk, June, if you keep running off with my kids? Open the door and let me see them."

Daddy smacks the door hard with his fists and cusses. I jump, startled. Inside, my heart is breaking.

Lucy screams in fear and hides behind me. I cry silently, wanting to open the door and hug my daddy, but knowing Mama will go off on me if I do. One time, I did race for the door. I couldn't stand not seeing him any longer.

"Daddy," I scream as I dash toward the door. "I love you, Daddy. Lucy and I want to come live with you. Get us out of here."

"Go to your room right now," Mama yells at me. "This is not your business."

"He's my daddy," I scream in defiance, a trait I would learn to perfect as I grew older, and one that would continue to get me into trouble.

Mama spins around and slaps my face so hard, I fall straight down to the ground. Daddy yells and pounds on the door. Lucy cries. Mama cusses and stomps her feet to the telephone. With my cheek throbbing and my vision blurry from tears, I pick up Lucy and we go into our bedroom. I slam the door shut.

Next thing I see out of my window are flashing red lights. She called the cops.

Shortly after that, we move. I never see him again. Everywhere we go, I search for his face in the crowd. I secretly hope I get one more hug or can nuzzle my head in his neck for one of those sniffs that make me feel safe.

Maybe he's in jail, maybe Mama outsmarted him, or maybe he stopped trying to find us because the drugs became more important. Drugs and alcohol may be eating him up, but I know my old daddy is in there somewhere.

2

A bump in the road jars me from my past back to Danny, who is not my daddy and never will be. I stare at the back of his head. He's developing a bald spot on the top and toward the back. Mix that with his long, wavy brown hair, which has been whipped in the wind of the half-opened car window, and he looks like a clown.

His hair usually looks a little greasy too, like he isn't quite sure what to do with a bottle of shampoo. His long mutton-chop sideburns and tinted glasses make me feel like he's trying to hide something. It might be the style, but on Danny it's creepy. My daddy would have called him a dip stick or a candyass. I giggle at the thought.

Sometimes, Danny looks at me and my sister with…I'm not sure what…contempt? Love? Not love, no…definitely not love! It's a scary mixture, whatever it is. It makes me uncomfortable, but I'm not sure why.

The boys at school look at me the same way. I can't ever tell if they hate me, like me or worse. Boys never tell you what they're thinking. Sometimes they're weird. Except for Ben. I like Ben. And he likes me too. He has a handsome smile like my daddy, and he makes my legs feel shaky when he's around. Sometimes it's hard to breathe.

Yesterday was the best and worst day of my life. I can never tell Mama or even Lucy what happened. Ben saw me walking home alone after school and caught up with me.

~

"Hey, Cart," Ben says. "Can I talk to you?"

"Sure," I say. I avert my eyes to the ground, peeking up only briefly. I could have died right then and there, his face being the last thing I ever see. I've secretly had a crush on him for a long time. I can't believe he wants to talk to me.

Next thing I know, he grabs my hand and drags me into a grove of apple trees not far from my house. He leans me against the trunk of a tree and lifts my chin with his hand and kisses me. He kisses me! His breath smells of mint gum and his skin of sweat, mixed with deodorant.

The kiss is soft and gentle and makes me dizzy. Then he kisses harder and more passionately as he pulls me in closer to him, holding me tight. I can feel every movement of his body against mine. My thoughts are foggy, and if somebody would ask me my name, I wouldn't know it. My breath catches in my throat as he pulls away from me and stands back. Words won't come. My eyes barely open. He searches my face for a clue of how I am feeling.

"I'm sorry," he says. "Do you hate me for doing that?"

I shake my head no. Then I run. For God's sake, I run. It is the only thing I can think to do. The kiss made it the best day and my running made it the worst day. I am such an idiot.

~

My eyes come back into focus. I realize I'm back in Danny's car, staring at the back of his clown head. Why in the hell did I run when Ben kissed me? I liked it. I liked it a lot. It took me off guard. I felt embarrassed and guilty for liking it. I didn't want to leave Ben, but I sure as hell didn't want to be loose like my mama.

Mama tells me to keep my legs closed no matter what sweet talking trash comes out of boys' mouths. Mama needs to wisen up and take her own advice. Danny needs to go away. And we need to go back home to Mason so Daddy can find us. I'm tired of moving around and not having friends to talk to about stuff.

I didn't get to tell Ben we were moving. He probably thinks I hate him. I want to go back to Mason. I want to tell Ben I don't hate him.

I look inside my macramé bag and find my Magic 8 Ball. I shake it, while still inside the bag, so no one will see. I whisper a question to it, "Will my mama EVER think with her head, keep her own legs closed, and put me and Lucy first? Oh, and dump that loser Danny so we can move back to Mason? And will I ever be able to tell Ben I don't hate him?"

I stop shaking the ball and look inside for my answer. *Very Doubtful,* stares back at me. My heart sinks. Maybe I asked it too many questions. I sigh, fighting back the tears that fill my eyes. A fat lot of help that was. I close the bag and look out the window.

The dust flying inside with the wind, cakes to my sticky, hot skin. I pull my thick hair back into a ponytail and secure it with a band from my wrist.

I look up at Mama in the front seat of the car. She's staring blankly out the window at the corn that is just starting to sprout in the fields. It's early yet. Around here they say knee high by the Fourth of July. It's only early June.

I wonder what Mama's thinking. I can't shake the fight I overheard she and Danny having in their bedroom last night. I don't think he wants Lucy and me to come along on this move. I heard him tell her to send us to relatives. I heard Mama say there aren't any relatives who'd take us in. She said something about not being able to leave us on a damn street corner, so we have to go with them. Just the kind of love you want to hear pouring out of your mama's mouth.

I want to plug my ears and scream. I don't know what's worse, the sound of their fighting or the sound of them fooling around when they make up. Both make me sick. Last night was no exception. I play hiding games with Lucy under the bedspread, hoping that the covers stop her from hearing them. She never asks, so I never offer an explanation. I feel like I have to protect her because I don't know if anyone else will.

I sneak a peek up at Danny as he's driving down the road. Through the rearview mirror, I catch him staring at me with cold, brown eyes. I can't read his expression. I never can. I jump when he clears his throat. He grins, like I'm afraid of him or something. Narrowing my gaze back at him, I recall this morning, before we left Mason.

~

"Everybody needs to get their asses in gear," Danny shouts, as he reaches for another box to take out to his friend Tommy's waiting truck.

Tommy works for U-Haul and is letting us use the truck for nothing. Except I'm sure he will get paid in beer later. I hate when Danny has his friends over and they drink beer. They make me uncomfortable.

Without thinking, I mutter, "Maybe you should leave us here and get your own ass moving."

I was sure he wasn't within earshot. I never thought the back of his hand across my cheek would smart as much as it did. He grins when he sees the look of horror on my face.

"Don't tempt me," Danny hisses, moving within inches of my face. "I'd have no problem leaving your ass here."

"Mama," I cry out, backing away from him.

"Aw, dammit, Cart," she says. "If you'd learn to keep your smart mouth shut, you'd go a lot farther in life. Danny

15

is trying to do right by us. Is it so hard to do what you're told?"

Of course, she takes his side.

"I don't have to listen to a damn thing he says. He's not my daddy, and never will be."

"Yeah, well your daddy don't want you either or he'd be here," Danny hisses. "And I'd gladly let him have you and your snot-nosed sister."

That's a low blow. I stomp off crying to my empty room. Slamming the door shut as hard as I can, I sink down onto the floor in a corner and sulk. Is it true? Would my daddy ever not want me? I don't know anymore. Mama comes in a few minutes later.

"Where is my daddy?" I ask through tears. "Can't Lucy and I go stay with him? I hate Danny. He's creepy and doesn't like us. I don't want to move with him."

"Cart, we don't have much of a choice," she says. "I don't know where your damn daddy is and I don't care. We have Danny now. He is all we need. He will take care of us."

I roll my eyes at her and look away. I want to hit her for being so stupid.

"Cart, it's time to go," she says, softening her voice a little. She bends down and half-smiles as she brushes my reddened cheek with her fingertips. I flinch at her touch.

"Can you try to be a little more cooperative?" she asks. "Your foul mouth comes straight from the gutter and is what gets you into trouble."

"Yeah, well, I wonder where I get it from," I say.

"McCartney Matthews, that's just the kind of attitude that gets you into trouble," Mama says.

She stands up and walks toward the door. I can't believe I don't get another smack across the face for the comment. Maybe she sees the truth in it. She turns and looks at me, arms folded across her chest.

16

"Just listen to Danny and behave. He's not that bad if you give him a chance. He's willing to take care of us, so we need to be grateful."

Grateful. He comes into our house, doesn't want Lucy and me around, smacks me and moves us to a strange town and I'm supposed to be grateful? He'll get a grateful chance from me when pigs fly and hell freezes straight over.

~

Letting go of this morning's nightmare, I drift back into the dusty car, and see Danny staring at me through the rearview mirror.

"You know you and Lucy have to share a bedroom and a bed at the new place, right, Cart?" Danny says, his angry, brown eyes darkening, daring me to say something. "The room is smaller and can only fit one bed. I told Tommy he could keep the other bed."

He grins at me. And it's not a friendly grin. It's almost like he's trying to get me to fight with him. I want to tell him I'll sleep in the dirt with a pit of snakes just to be away from him, but he'd probably make me.

Besides, I don't know where we are and I don't want to risk getting tossed out of the car. He'd do it and Mama would probably let him. I'll never leave Lucy with them. Danny is nothing like Daddy. Daddy's smile makes me smile and I'd never think of being a smart mouth to him. Danny's smiles are empty. I've never seen someone smile with their mouth while their eyes stay cold, hard and flat. A smile is not supposed to feel like a threat. How can I make my mama see that?

"Fine, Danny," I hiss and look away.

Danny looks over to Mama and smacks her on the shoulder.

17

"Do you hear how she talks to me?" he yells. "It's bullshit, June. She better learn to show me respect and keep that smart mouth of hers shut."

"She said fine, Danny. Lighten up." Mama shoots me a harsh look.

"Your tone is going to get you more than what you bargain for one day, Miss Attitude," Danny says.

His eyes pierce straight through me. A cold shiver runs up my spine. I look down at my mood ring. It's black.

He floors the gas pedal and all of our heads jerk back. He laughs, deep and loud. It is empty and hollow, like his smiles.

Lucy begins to stir. Gratefully, I turn my gaze toward her and away from Danny and my icy black ring. I don't know what Danny would do. I vow to make sure I am never alone with him to find out.

3

About an hour later, we cruise into a town. I barely catch the name on the sign as we fly by. Freeport, I think it says. Why does that sound familiar? Danny doesn't slow down much when we hit the city limits. That is, until he sees a cop and slows to 30. He waves. The cop nods, but eyes him suspiciously as we drive by.

I can already tell this place is much smaller than Mason. It's a Sunday afternoon and everything we pass by seems to be closed. Daddy always says the only places open on a Sunday in our neck of the woods are churches, movie theaters and gas stations. Looks like Freeport is the same.

We drive through the downtown area and pass by a plaza. It has a large, marble water fountain on one end, and a life-sized, stone dolphin on the other end. A group of kids laugh and climb on the dolphin, their parents sitting on nearby benches, visiting with each other. What I wouldn't give to have a normal family. There are lots of shops and restaurants along the plaza that are closed. I wonder if we can get Mama to bring us down here sometime to look around.

A few minutes later, we turn on a street called Float and pull up in front of a small two-story house. Dirty, white siding, with grimy yellow shutters, a rickety front porch and a large yellow door, stare back at us. Yellow is my least favorite color. I'm not sure why, but it is.

I'd like to float on out of here and go back home, or anywhere that Danny isn't. Fat chance that's going to happen. Danny shuts the car off and we all sit there for a minute.

"Here we are," Danny says, breaking the silence. "Our new crib."

"Oh, Danny," Mama gushes. She reaches over and hugs him. "It's bitchin'. Let's go check it out before Tommy gets here with our stuff."

Mama, Danny, Lucy and I pile out of the car. Danny leads the way as we walk up the wooden steps and cross the sagging porch. He pulls open the aluminum screen door and unlocks the ugly, yellow front door, pushing it open to reveal the inside. As we enter into the living room, the aluminum door slams shut with a thud behind Lucy. I quickly switch spots with her and stand closest to the door. Danny turns and scowls at me.

"What the hell, Cart?" Danny yells.

"Sorry, how am I supposed to know it slams shut like that?" I ask.

"Well, don't do it again," he says, scowling.

Turning back around, he wraps his arm around Mama's back, reaching down giving her butt a squeeze. Mama giggles and slaps him lightly, like she doesn't like it. I roll my eyes and look away, wishing I could block Lucy from seeing that.

Lucy turns and hugs me, gratitude showing in her eyes. She feels the same way about Danny as I do. Neither of us can shake the bad vibe he gives off. Why can't Mama pick up on that?

Danny gives us the grand tour of his crappy crib. On the first floor, there is a living room, dining room and kitchen. Scratched and dull hard wood cover the floors in the living room and dining room. Dirty, threadbare, area rugs grace the center of each of the rooms. The kitchen is the worst. It's small, with gray and white linoleum floors and greasy cabinets and walls.

As we walk back through the dining and living room, I spy the stairs that go to the second floor.

"Come on, Cart," Lucy says, spying the stairs too. "Let's find our room." Lucy counts the steps as we climb.

Danny calls out from below, "The room at the top of the landing is yours."

Lucy and I head toward the room, anticipating the same greatness we saw on the first floor. We stumble to a halt. It is yellow. Yellow. Ain't that the shits?

I roll my eyes as we step inside the room. It's small, with worn blue carpet. One tiny, high window lets in a small amount of light. I peek into the closet. That's disappointing. It will be a challenge to fit my clothes, let alone Lucy's. We'll have to share a dresser too, as there will only be room for one. This is the tiniest excuse for a bedroom I have ever seen.

"We'll have to see if we can get some paint to make your walls a different color," Mama says, entering the room. "I know yellow isn't your favorite."

"Pink would be cool," I say, smiling.

Wow. Mama is willing to do something nice. I step up on my tiptoes, and look out that tiny, high window, to see if I can see hell freezing over.

"There's nothing wrong with yellow walls. Paint costs money. Do you have money?" Danny asks, moving to stand in the doorway.

He's sneaky. I didn't hear him come up the steps. That could be a problem.

"No," I say.

"Yeah, that's what I thought," he replies. "The yellow stays."

Mama shrugs her shoulders. "You'll get used to it, Cart. Maybe you'll even grow to love the color yellow."

There's the mama we all know and love. Once again, she takes his side. I'll like yellow and Danny about the same time. Never. I'd like to take the Magic 8 Ball out of my bag and chuck it at the back of Danny's balding, clown head, but that would be a huge waste of a great 8 Ball.

As Lucy and I leave our room, we peek into the bathroom, to the right of our bedroom. It has a sink, a tub and a toilet that needs a good scrubbing. And the walls are pink. Figures. Maybe I'll look in the basement and see if there's any pink paint left down there for our bedroom. Danny walks us down the long hallway that separates their bedroom from ours. It's gigantic with lots of windows and that fancy brown paneling that's so popular. The windows need shining and the paneling could use a good scrubbing. I bet four beds could easily fit into this room.

"This is our private haven," Danny says, squeezing Mama and then, turning to glance at me and Lucy, "as in your mama's and mine. No kids allowed. Can you dig it?"

"That's fine with me," I answer, rolling my eyes.

I turn and glance out of the window and see Tommy pulling up with the U-Haul. He lays on the horn.

"Let's get our stuff in here," Danny says.

As he passes by me, he brushes my arm, giving me a slight pinch. I flinch backward. He tilts his head so Mama can't see and grins at me. He acts like nothing happened.

"Tommy and I will get the heavy stuff. You chicks get the cleaning stuff out and make this place sparkle."

"I'll make sure the beer is nice and chilled for when you're done, baby," Mama calls to him, as he heads down the stairs. "Ok, girls, let's get this house in shape. We want Danny to know we can earn our keep."

Just as I figure, Lucy and I end up scrubbing, polishing, and shining that whole house, except for Danny and Mama's room. They said we are not allowed in there. Fine with me. Mama manages to run around looking busy as hell but not doing a single thing.

Meanwhile, Lucy and I have fun hanging the dirty area rugs over the line out back and beating the dust out of them. We pretend they are Danny and pummel the crap out of them while laughing.

We go back inside to see what else needs to be done and find Mama hiding out in the kitchen reading a magazine. Danny and Tommy are hauling in furniture, putting it in the appropriate rooms. We make sure whatever room Danny is in, we aren't.

We scrub the grease off the kitchen cabinets and counters. It turns out the linoleum in the kitchen wasn't gray and white. It was only dirty. Now it's dull, white and scratched, but at least it's clean.

The bathroom also sparkles and you could eat off any of the floors if you wanted to, but that's gross. I remember hearing Mama say that expression once, but I can't imagine it was after anything she cleaned.

"June," Danny says, squeezing my mama a little too long. "You have done a groovy job making this house sparkle."

"Oh, well you know the girls helped," Mama says, hugging Danny and winking over his shoulder at Lucy and me.

I scowl at Mama, but she acts like she doesn't see it. She knows damn well she hasn't lifted a pinky finger to clean anything. But, she made sure Danny saw her with a bucket in her hand and a towel over her shoulder while he was hauling in furniture. Mama is very good at deceiving people.

"I see you missed the windows and paneling in our bedroom though," Danny adds, frowning down at Mama.

"Really?" Mama answers. "I sent the girls up there to take care of it while I scrubbed in the kitchen."

"You never," I begin to say, but she holds her finger to her mouth, as Danny turns to look at me. He crosses his arms and gives me a foul look.

"You told us we aren't allowed in there, so I figured you'd clean your own room," I blurt out, immediately wishing I could take it back.

Danny's face reddens and his eyes darken. He squeezes both of his hands into fists and holds them at his sides. I take a step backward, my eyes never leaving his. Lucy moves to stand behind me, eyes wide with terror.

"I wouldn't think twice about putting you over my knee and spanking your disrespectful ass, do you understand?" Danny half-screams. "You are in MY house now and you WILL listen to me or you're going to be one miserable little brat. Got it?"

I stare at Danny and Mama. I can't believe she sold me out again. I refuse to let them see me cry. Mama walks over to me with the bucket of cleaning water and window spray and hands it to me. She can't look me in the eye.

"Be a doll and help out, Cart," Mama says. "Then you and Lucy can go exploring for a bit. Danny's going to set the grill up and we'll have burgers later."

She finally looks at me and I give her the meanest look I can muster as I take the items from her. She quickly averts her gaze. I turn toward the stairs as a single tear slides from my eye.

"I'll help you, Cart," Lucy says, grabbing paper towels and a couple of rags. As we climb the stairs, Lucy says, "I saw a school down the street with a playground and toys. Let's go down there when we finish."

"Anywhere but here," I say, as we enter the "haven."

Lucy works on the lower windows and walls as I reach for the higher ones. We complete the job in silence. I don't know what to say. I usually try to keep positive and not share too much with Lucy. She's so young.

Mama never betrayed me before Danny came along, well at least not quite this bad. I know she has pulled some tricks regarding my daddy. Now, I'm wondering just how bad those tricks were.

I think Daddy used to talk about Freeport. Maybe that's why the sign looks familiar. Did he say his mother lives here somewhere? I can't remember for sure. It was so long ago. Even if she does, I'm not sure I want to find her or she wants us to find her. She sounds mean and unloving. Could it be any worse than Danny though?

An hour later, Lucy and I come downstairs. I see Mama and Danny sitting on the front porch with Tommy. While we were upstairs scrubbing the room we are never supposed to go into, they're outside drinking beer. Next time, they can clean their own bedroom.

I take a quick look around my new home. The living room furniture is set in place, along with the table and chairs in the dining room, all freshly polished. We walk into the kitchen. It looks and smells clean. There is a small table and two chairs in the corner. Danny already told us that Lucy and I will eat in the kitchen and they will eat in the dining room. He sure is hell bent on separating us. So much for being a family. I hope he rots in hell. I take my macramé bag from the counter and throw it over my shoulder.

I hear the U-Haul engine come to life. It's so loud, you can probably hear it fire up in Mason. The front screen door slams shut with a thud. Mama and Danny are laughing. Lucy and I walk back into the living room. Danny's hands are all over Mama, copping a feel and she is letting him. Over Mama's shoulder, he spots us.

"We're taking a little break from unpacking," he says, looking back at Mama, smiling. "Why don't you kids go play in the street for awhile?"

"Danny," Mama says with a giggle, "you're so silly." She swats at his shoulder, still giggling.

"We're going to the school playground," I say. "We'll be back later."

"Take your time," Danny yells, swatting Mama on the butt as he chases her up the stairs.

I turn toward Lucy, with a weak smile. "I put a package of cookies in the cupboard by the stove. Let's get them and go on an adventure."

"Ok, Cart," Lucy replies and then, pauses to look at me.

I can't quite read her expression. I hope she doesn't ask me too many questions about Mama and Danny. I'm not sure how to answer them.

"I'm glad I have you," she says.

She squeezes me and a knot forms in my throat so big, I almost can't breathe. I hug her back even tighter, kissing the top of her curly, blonde head.

4

Lucy and I munch on cookies in silence as we walk toward the school. If there are kids to play with in this neighborhood, we don't see any.

"Cart," Lucy says, swallowing her cookie. "How long is Mama going to be with Danny?"

"I don't know. She doesn't seem to stay with them for very long."

"Does she love him?"

"I don't know if Mama is capable of loving anyone but herself."

"So, why is she with him?"

"Some people are afraid to be alone," I say. "They need a man on their arm in order to have self-worth."

"How do you know these things?"

"Mama got a pamphlet from the Community Health Center after her break-up with Frank. She left it on her nightstand one day and I saw it when I was dusting, so I read it."

"Ooooh, I didn't like Frank. He smelled like beer and needed a bath."

I laugh.

"It's kind of how they all smell, Lucy."

"What was my daddy like?" she asks. "I don't remember too much about him."

"You would have loved Daddy," I tell her. My eyes light up and a smile spreads clear across my face. "Well, the old Daddy, anyway."

"What does that mean?"

"Before the war and before things started going bad, Daddy was so much fun! He loved to laugh and joke around. And his smile! His smile was so handsome you couldn't help but smile back at him. And it reached all the way to his eyes. It was like his eyes were smiling at you, too. Not like Danny, whose smile never leaves his lips. There's something dark and unfriendly lurking in Danny's eyes. Daddy's eyes were bright and shiny and full of life. They also held a bit of naughty. But the good, fun kind of naughty. I remember one time he bought fake plastic dog poop at the store and left it on Mama's chair at the kitchen table. She screamed when she pulled out her chair to sit down and a pile of poop stared back at her."

Lucy wrinkles her nose. "That's kind of gross."

"It was gross," I say, smiling, "but since it wasn't real, it was funny, too. And Daddy loved music. He only listened to the Beatles. He has all of their records. He'd put a record on the turntable; hold you in one arm, while moving the needle over to the record with his free hand. When the music would start to play, I'd race up and stand on his feet, wrapping my arms around his waist. We'd all three dance around the living room. It was so much fun."

"That sounds like fun. Do you know where his records are? Could you and I do that sometime?"

"I don't know where they are. I haven't seen them or the bobbleheads since he left."

"Cart?" Lucy stops walking and turns toward me. "Will you shake your Magic 8 Ball and ask if our daddy is ever coming back?"

I stop walking and turn toward Lucy. I pause for a long time, staring down at the sidewalk. I try holding in the tears. I've shaken that Magic 8 Ball a million times and asked if my daddy was coming home, and every time it says, *Reply Hazy, Try Again.* Every time.

"I'm afraid to," I say. "What if it says something I don't want to see?"

"We need to know," Lucy says.

Brave Lucy. I reach inside my bag for the Magic 8 Ball. I close my eyes and shake it with all of the hope and love I can muster. "Is our daddy coming back home?"

I open my eyes and look inside. My heart sinks.

Reply Hazy. Try Again.

I show it to Lucy.

"Is it broken?" she asks.

"No, it says other things all the time."

"Ask it if this is a nice town."

"Is this a good town to live in?" I shook the Magic 8 Ball again, secretly hoping it *was* broken.

As I See It, Yes.

Lucy grabs the 8 Ball from me and frantically shakes it. "Are we ever going to see our daddy?"

Reply Hazy. Try Again.

Lucy hands me the Magic 8 Ball, lowers her head and stares at the sidewalk for a long time. I want to throw it into the middle of the street and hope a semi runs over it, smashing it to tiny little pieces. Instead, I stick it back in my bag and sigh.

"At least it didn't say no. Maybe that's a good sign," Lucy says, reaching up to hold my hand. She begins walking again, pulling me along.

"So, tell me, what other things did Daddy do with us?"

"Daddy used to take us to the park, push us on the swings, and then we'd go for ice cream. You probably don't remember that though. You were still in a stroller. Mama didn't go with us too often. I don't know what she did while we were gone but a lot of times when we'd get back, Daddy would send us upstairs and tell me to read you stories. I could hear them arguing. When Mama's around, there's always arguing."

"That much I *do* know," Lucy says.

~

After returning from the school playground, we eat dinner, or at least attempt to anyway. Danny did make burgers on the grill, but he and Mama paid more attention to drinking beer and each other than they did to burger flipping. Crunchy burgers aren't appealing.

I might push my luck in the smart mouth department when Danny's sober, but I learned quickly when he's drinking, he's way more dangerous.

Lucy and I bury those crispy hockey pucks in ketchup and half a can of baked beans and eat them without saying a word. We excuse ourselves and go up to our room, saying we have boxes to unpack.

Later that evening, Mama knocks on our door and comes in. She is pretty hammered.

"We're out of beer," Mama says, slurring her words almost to the point of not understanding them. "We're heading over to one of Danny's friend's for a while. Damn liquor laws of no selling beer or having open bars on Sundays."

"Ok," I say. "Have fun."

Mama blows a half-assed kiss, turns and stumbles towards the stairs. I'm thinking if you're drunk and run out of beer, maybe you should go to bed. But that's not how they do things. Danny works second shift at his manufacturing job, so drinking late into the night never seems to be a problem for him.

When I hear the screen door slam shut, I know Mama and Danny are gone. That door might come in handy after all. I'll hear them coming and going. Relieved, Lucy and I lay back on the bed.

"Let's listen to my radio," I tell Lucy.

"That sounds like fun," she says. "I love listening to music."

I get up and go to the closet. I keep my transistor radio hidden on the top shelf. I bring it back to the bed and sit down. Mama bought it for my last birthday. She never does stuff like that. I didn't question why, I was just so happy to get one. It's light blue with a matching blue wrist strap.

I turn the knob and it clicks on to the sound of static. I pull the antennae up as far as it will go and turn the tuner until we hear music.

"Dancing Queen!" Lucy and I both yell out.

I turn the radio up as loud as it will go and we jump off of the bed. Lucy comes over to me and places her feet on top of my feet, like I used to do with Daddy. We laugh and dance around the room until the song is over. We crash back on the bed, trying to catch our breath. I turn the radio off so we don't use up all of the battery.

"That was fun!" Lucy exclaims.

"It feels good to laugh and dance and be a kid," I answer. "I wish Mama and Danny would go out more often."

"Me, too," Lucy says, and then frowns. "Cart, Danny is creepy."

"I know," I say. "Just stay away from him as much as you can. And try never to be alone with him."

I don't know what else to say or what we can do to change anything.

"Let's get ready for bed. It's getting late."

"Ok," Lucy answers. Her voice seems to hold a certain disappointment at my lack of good answers.

We put our pajamas on, turn the light off, and get settled in bed. There isn't a whole lot of room for both of us in the twin bed but I like having Lucy close to me. It makes me feel like I'm keeping her safe.

"Cart?" Lucy asks. "Can you tell me about how Daddy named me?"

"Yeah, I can tell you," I answer.

I smile as I recall Daddy's story. I see Lucy's eyes sparkling from the street light that's trickling in through the tiny window.

"It's no secret that Daddy loves the Beatles."

"Everybody knows that," Lucy says. "Unless they're dumb."

"Danny probably doesn't know it," I say.

Lucy and I laugh. Danny could get bit square on the butt by a smart bug and no intelligence would seep through.

"Ok, so, two weeks before you were born, the Beatles came out with the song, *Lucy in the Sky with Diamonds.* Daddy loved that song so much. He said it appealed to his sense of silly and said everyone should have a sense of silly within them. It makes life bearable and entertaining. Daddy said when you were born you had a head full of wild, blonde hair and the most beautiful kaleidoscope eyes, just like the Lucy in the song. And, he swore on a stack of Bibles you smiled at him. Mama told him newborn babies don't smile. But Daddy knew you smiled just for him. So, with your beautiful smile and sparkly eyes, he insisted they name you Lucy."

"I love that story, Cart," Lucy says, smiling at the thought of her daddy.

"When you got bigger, Daddy would take us both outside to play. He'd toss you up in the air, and then catch you as you came back down. You'd giggle and giggle. When he had you in mid-air, he'd sing 'Lucy in the sky with diamonds', and you'd sing 'ooooohhhhhhhh.' It was so funny and entertaining. He really did name you perfectly."

I tickle Lucy and give her a big bear hug. She smiles up at me with her beautiful multi-colored eyes.

"I wish I could remember more about Daddy," Lucy says. "Can you tell me another story about him?"

"Sure," I say. "My favorite, is when Daddy still lived with us and he'd come into our bedroom and tuck us in at night.

He'd sing the Beatles Lullaby song, *Golden Slumbers*. I'm sure you don't remember it. You were a baby. But, maybe I can hum it for you."

"Ok, Cart," Lucy says, yawning. "That sounds nice."

Lucy snuggles in close to me. I wrap my arms around her like our daddy used to do with me. I hum the song softly, as I twirl the curls on top of her head. I get lost in the memories as I hum. I dream it's my daddy who is singing to me. I dream it's *his* arms around me, holding me.

My voice cracks with sobs. I open my eyes and look down at Lucy. Her eyes are closed. I hear slow and steady breathing. The corners of her mouth turn upward, smiling, even as she sleeps.

I close my eyes again, but the tears still escape and trail down my cheeks, falling softly into her hair. Daddy has to be out there somewhere. I want to know what happened to him. I *need* to know what happened to him.

5

A couple of days later, Lucy and I make a plan to sneak into the basement when Danny leaves for work. It's supposed to be his day off, but he's been called in for extra hours. That's fine by us. Lucy's plan is to make this trip to the basement a 'dangerous mission.' I play along but really only want to find some pink paint from the bathroom, or any color other than yellow.

We creep down the stairs from our bedroom, cutting through the dining room, careful not to disturb Mama in the living room. She's working hard, lounging on the couch with her favorite magazine in one hand and a beer in the other. She doesn't see us. Honestly, she could look right at us and still not see us. But for Lucy's sake, we keep creeping along on our 'dangerous mission.'

As we make our way through the kitchen, we zero in on the basement door. Lifting the hook and eye latch, I open the door and lead the way. I turn and close the door firmly behind us, once Lucy has come through. Flipping on the light switch, I notice a few steps down, there is a landing and a side door. There are hooks on the wall opposite of the door for hanging coats. I'm sure this side door is where Danny will expect us to come in this winter with our snowy boots, winter coats, hats and gloves. God forbid we track snow into his crib. I bet if he could get away with it, he'd make us live and sleep in the basement, like unwanted pets. Yeah, he'd probably like that a whole bunch.

Lucy and I descend a handful more of rickety, old wooden steps and reach the bottom.

"I hate open steps like that," Lucy says, shuddering. "Open steps scare me. I don't want to fall through or have someone reach through and grab my ankles."

"You won't fall through," I reassure her. "And no one will grab your ankles either. That stuff only happens in the movies."

I'm not sure Lucy feels reassured, so I pull the bag off my shoulder and reach inside for my Magic 8 Ball. Both rarely leave my side. I shake it up and with a twinkle in my eye, I ask it if Lucy will fall through the open steps, or if anyone will grab her ankles as she comes down to the basement. I look over at Lucy, who is holding her breath. As I peek inside, Lucy's eyes grow wide with anticipation. I show her the answer.

My Sources Say No.

Lucy sighs with relief.

I laugh.

"See? I told you!"

With that problem solved, I put the 8 Ball back in my bag and take a quick look around the musty, limestone-walled basement. In the center of the room stands a large, old furnace with pipes extending to all parts of the house. I hope this thing works. Winters in Illinois are cold. I see a coal chute door on the wall. I hope it's not still in use. I can see Lucy and me down here shoveling coal while the wardens scream from upstairs that they're cold, not that I'm dramatic or anything.

In the corner, to the right of the furnace, is a wooden work bench and in the corner to the left of the furnace sits an old washer and dryer with a work sink next to it. I'm sure Mama will have me figuring how to work it soon enough. She won't make the effort, but she'll make sure Danny thinks it's her doing the laundry. At least we won't be getting dumped off at the laundromat anymore. She says she'll be right back and never is. Lucy and I spend the time playing Rock, Paper, Scissors, or shaking the 8 Ball and asking it all sorts of silly questions. Hours later, she'll turn up reeking of alcohol.

Lucy and I head toward the work bench first. On top, sit a few dusty baby food jars filled with various nails, screws and washers. I'll have to remember the nails if I ever plan to hang anything on our bedroom walls, even though Danny has said we can't put a bunch of nail holes in *his* walls. The walls are not where I'd like to put a bunch of nail holes, if he wants to know the truth.

Lucy digs around under the bench and finds a cardboard box filled with paint cans. There's an old, stiff brush in the box along with a paint can opener. Lucy and I lift the cans to check for color and swish them to see if they still hold liquid or if they're dried up.

"Cart, look!" Lucy yells, lifting up a paint can that has pink on the outside.

She holds it up like it's the golden ticket inside the chocolate bar of Willie Wonka and the Chocolate Factory. She swishes the can and we hear liquid. I take the can opener and pry off the lid.

"I think it's still good, Lucy."

I put the lid back on the paint can and set it down as I pick up the brush. "You keep digging to see if there are any fun colors to go with it, and I'll wet this brush over at the sink and see if we can soften it up enough to use."

A short while later, Lucy and I are sneaking up the steps, toting two cans of paint, pink and green, along with a paintbrush whose bristles are sort of soft, but mostly hard. We stifle giggles so Mama can't hear us as we sneak through the dining room.

Before heading up to our bedroom, I shoo Lucy ahead of me and peek back at Mama on the couch. She's sound asleep with a magazine laying over her chest and an empty beer bottle sitting on the floor next to her. I'd like to say I am surprised to see her like this but it happens more often than not. Especially once Danny leaves for work. She'll probably ask us to clean something later or figure out how to use the washer and dryer downstairs. She'll tell Danny she did all of the work. One day he'll figure it out, but he's not too bright, so it could take some time.

"Cart?" Lucy asks, once inside our room with the door closed. "How are we going to paint our room? Do you think Danny will get mad? Do we have enough paint?"

Laughing, I say, "Lucy, slow down! There's not much paint left in these cans, so maybe we can paint different shapes or something. The walls will still have to be mostly yellow, but the pink and green will make it look cool."

"Oh, that's a great idea," Lucy says, sitting down on the bed to watch.

I paint a big, pink circle with a peace sign in the middle, on the wall at the foot of our bed. When we wake up in the morning, it'll be the first thing we see. Hopefully, it'll help us think calm, peaceful thoughts. I add a few squares and diamonds with a pink and green pattern in various spots around the room. The brush is still pretty hard but does a decent enough job.

"Oooh, that one looks like a diamond Easter egg," Lucy exclaims, pointing to the wall.

"Pretty cool, isn't it?" I say, standing back, admiring my work. "We have to have a diamond for our very own Lucy in the Sky with Diamonds!"

"I love you Cart."

Lucy comes up behind me and wraps her arms around my waist, hugging herself to my back. I close my eyes, hold onto her arms, and soak up the feeling of being loved. Sometimes, that feeling makes me want to cry, but I think it's a good cry. It's a feeling I've only ever felt from Lucy and Daddy.

By the time I finish painting the designs, there is just enough pink and green shapes on the walls to take the edge off the yellow. In fact, it makes me not mind that ugly yellow so much at all.

Lucy and I put the lids on the paint, wash the brush out in the bathroom sink, and then sneak back downstairs. As we round the corner, Mama is standing at the sink in the kitchen. Darn it. I forgot to see if she was still on the couch. She turns toward us before we can sneak back out.

"What's going on?" Mama asks, looking at us and then down at the cans of paint in our hands. "What in the hell did you two do? Danny is not going to be happy you painted on his walls."

Lucy sinks in behind me.

"I found some old pink and green paint in the basement and thought I'd decorate our room. Just a little bit. We didn't paint the walls completely."

Mama eyes me skeptically. "What do you mean a little bit?"

"We'll put these paint cans back downstairs and show you. I think you'll like it. We do," I say, as cheery as I can, hoping my enthusiasm rubs off.

Lucy and I take the cans downstairs and by the time we get back up, Mama is already in our room looking around.

"Well?" I ask, watching Mama, trying to gauge her reaction.

"The colors are pretty with the yellow," Mama says, "although I'm not sure what Danny is going to say, but the shapes are cute. You have talent with the paint. I'll tell him I helped you, that way he won't be mad."

I hear Lucy's huge sigh of relief. I am a bit more hesitant of Mama's intentions, but I don't share that with Lucy. Why worry her. Is Mama saying she helped so Danny will think she's a hard worker? And what if he doesn't like it? Will she still be on our side? I feel this isn't going to end in our favor.

6

Later that night I hear the front door slam. Danny is home. That slamming door is either going to be a blessing or a curse. My anxiety grows as I sit up in bed, taking several deep breaths to calm myself. I'm sure Mama will tell Danny what we did. I hope she puts a positive spin on it.

It's late and Lucy has woken up and wandered off to the bathroom. I don't want a confrontation with Danny. Please Lucy, hurry up and get back here.

I turn the light switch on and reach over the side of the bed, pulling my Magic 8 Ball out of my bag. I shake it.

"Is Danny gonna be mad and is Mama going to throw us to the wolves again?" I ask it.

I peer inside cautiously as my guts wind into a big, old messed up knot. *Better Not Tell You Now* stuck in my throat like a basketball.

Hurry up and get back here Lucy, I scream silently. I don't want her meeting Danny in the hallway and him scaring her or worse yet, hurting her. I listen for Danny, my ears at full alert. Unfortunately, I don't have to wait long.

The next thing I know, Danny is leaping up the steps and throws open the door. I jump up and stand next to my bed, fear crushing my chest. My head throbs. Tears are already stinging my eyes.

"What in the hell is this shit?" he screams, looking around at the pink and green designs covering the walls.

"We just want to make our room look prettier," I say, facing Danny as bravely as I can. My heart is pounding out of control. I try sucking in a deep breath of air to calm myself, but it sticks in my throat.

My meek voice barely sputters out, "We didn't make a mess or drip on the carpet. The paint is not hurting anything. Even Mama says it looks nice. Ask her."

Danny lunges toward me. Screaming, I hold up my arms in self-defense, just as Lucy comes walking back into our bedroom.

"Cart!" Lucy screams.

She stands frozen in place.

Danny turns from me and goes after Lucy instead. I leap over the bed and jump between them. A fierce, protective force roars up inside of me.

"I will kill you dead and spit on your decaying body before I'll ever let you lay a single finger on my sister."

The rage I feel at the thought of him ever hurting Lucy, makes me feel like I *could* kill him dead. It's kind of scary what rage can do to a person.

Lucy screams hysterically and hides further behind me. Mama finally gets off her lazy butt and comes up the steps to intervene.

"Danny," Mama says, coming into our room. She stands next to him and strokes his arm.

"I didn't know what the girls were doing. I was busy cleaning the kitchen, but the paint didn't cost us nothing. They found it in the basement. Come on, let's go downstairs and I'll make you a sandwich and get you a beer. We can talk about your night at work. I'll give you a shoulder rub and we'll see what else happens."

She hugs Danny from behind and rubs herself up against him. He seems to calm down. He turns toward Mama, but then swings back around and slaps my face hard with the back of his hand. I stumble backward. My eyes immediately tear up. That flipping hurt like hell. Lucy gasps and Mama stands there with no expression registering on her face. I can feel my cheek growing hot and red from the impact.

"Don't *ever* do anything in this house again without my permission," he says.

Spit sprays from Danny's mouth. His eyes are as black as a moonless night. I shiver. His anger frightens the hell out of me.

"And if you *ever* talk to me like that again," he screams, mere inches from my face, "I will beat you. Do you understand that?"

My legs feel like they're going to give out and I falter in front of him. He grins.

"And I'll enjoy every damn minute of it, too," he says, poking me in the shoulder with his grubby finger.

We stand face to face, eyes locked, mine blinking rapidly. Time feels like it stopped. Nobody moves. Then he leans his body in toward me. I jump back, not knowing what he's going to do. I watch his lip twitch with satisfaction and then curl up at the corner.

He turns and stomps down the steps. Mama turns briefly to look at me. I cross my arms over my chest and narrow my glance at her, refusing to cry while she watches me.

"Say something, Mama," I spit out, choking back my tears. "What happened to telling him you helped us so he wouldn't be mad? Do you give a tiny little crap about me or Lucy?"

"There is really no sense in him being pissed at all of us," she says.

And with that, she turns and dutifully follows Danny down the stairs.

7

Lucy's eleventh birthday was a week ago and no one remembered but me. I snuck down to Woolworth's, with the little bit of money I had saved for a battery for my transistor radio, and bought her a cute peace ring. It has since tarnished her finger, but she loves it just the same. I also picked up a frosted, smiley-face cookie from the bakery and sang happy birthday to her.

Mama and Danny went out drinking that night. It still hasn't registered with her that she missed Lucy's birthday.

As I round up everyone's dirty laundry and take to the basement, I overhear Danny yelling at Mama about how he's tired of all of his hard-earned money going to feed us ungrateful kids and how the electric and water bills are higher with us around. I think if Einstein did the math, he'd see that most of his hard-earned money is going for beer.

And little does he know it isn't Mama who cooks up the crap he buys. It's me and Lucy. Wouldn't he be surprised to find out his precious June would screw up boiling water.

And yet, I hear Mama say she has nowhere else to send us, so we have to stay. She should be grateful Lucy and I are here and make her look good. She should think about defending us instead of wishing we'd go away. Maybe we should stop doing everything for her so Danny sees what she's really like. He'd send us packing in a heart beat. A girl can dream.

I have not made eye contact with Danny since the night he hit me. It's hard to look at someone who hates you so much they wish you were gone. The more I ignore him, the more it seems like he's trying to start a fight. I think he wants to have a reason to hurt me. I also think he's not going to wait for one. One of these days, the opportunity is going to present itself and he's going to do something.

I take my Magic 8 Ball out when Lucy isn't nearby and ask it if Danny wants to hurt us and make us go away. *Signs Point to Yes.* Great.

I decide Lucy and I need to do some exploring around town so we don't have a chance to irritate Danny. Especially on the days he's home. It's obvious he doesn't want us around. I think he looks forward to the times we are gone so he and Mama can run upstairs together. Not that he'd wait for us to be gone to do so. I'm just grateful they go upstairs and don't do it right there on the couch. That would be traumatizing. I can't imagine what it'd do to Lucy.

I don't get Mama's attraction to him. He doesn't bathe regularly and has bad breath. He drinks too much and too often. His greasy hair is gross. I'm sure he's peed out more than a few of his brain cells. You'd think he'd want to work real hard on hanging onto those scarce little fellas.

I also don't like the way he looks at Lucy and me. Something is brewing in that shallow head of his; I just don't know what it is. I hope we never find out. I hope Mama slips up and he finds out she doesn't do anything and we get the boot.

Lucy and I've been getting into the habit of pushing the back of the chair under the door knob of our room at night so he can't get in. At least we hope he can't. It helps us feel safer, anyway.

Sometimes, Mama gives us a couple of dollars to disappear for a while. Danny never gives us money. He boots us out and could care less if we don't have money, are hungry, or it's raining. And we've been booted out many, many times. At least it's been warm so far. I'm not sure what we'll do when it gets cold out. Maybe the library is open long hours in the winter. I've been able to teach Lucy how to jump rope, play hopscotch and cross the monkey bars at the school down the street. She's so good now she can skip every other bar.

We pretty much know where everything is in Freeport now, too. On the days Mama gives us money, we browse around Woolworth's, the store downtown where I got Lucy's peace ring. They have everything in this store.

Today, we decide to save our money for something better. Ice cream. When we leave the store, we walk over to the Union Dairy and each get a single vanilla cone. After that, we do some window shopping on Main Street. Women's and men's shops, a bookstore, a drugstore, along with a couple of restaurants and a movie theater, line the old cobblestone streets. Tiny red-leafed trees and big barrels of colorful flowers decorate the sidewalks. It's beautiful.

On the days it's super hot and sunny, we dip our arms in the cool water of the marble fountain on the plaza and splash our faces. The sign says to stay out but it feels good to cool off, so we do it anyway. What's the purpose of having a water fountain, if you can't use it to cool off?

Sometimes, we walk by the theater and admire the posters on the outside walls, advertising what's playing. I hope one day Lucy and I can scrounge up enough money to see a movie. I think any money Mama gives us from now on we'll save for a movie. It'll be something fun to do when it starts getting cold out.

I remember Daddy taking us to a movie once when we were younger. He let me get popcorn and pop. Lucy was little and slept through the whole thing. I don't remember what we watched, but I remember feeling special and loved.

Rocky is playing at this movie theater. I've never cared much for violent movies but maybe I could pick up some good *Rocky* moves to use on Danny.

Or maybe we could buy some books at the bookstore and read up on martial arts or self-defense. I remember Daddy reading to me, but those books were fun stories like *The Cat in the Hat.* I never thought I'd have to read books on self-defense.

Sometimes, when Lucy and I are downtown, we sit on the bench by the stone dolphin and people watch. If there aren't many people around, Lucy plays on the dolphin. If there are a lot of people nearby, she stays close to me, afraid to wander off too far. It makes me sad that she has such a fear of other people. I blame Mama and Danny for that. I hope one day they get what's coming to them.

I'm glad Freeport is small enough that we can walk everywhere. Mason, where we came from, was too big. We'd have to take a bus or cab but there was never money for that. So we never went farther than we could walk or ride our bikes, which did not make the cut to Freeport. Danny sold them, just to be mean, I think.

Lucy and I have found some great parks while exploring Freeport. She likes it when we go to the parks. Read Park has a huge pool. I hope we can swim there sometime. The smaller parks have swings, slides and teeter totters.

But, the really big park, Krape Park, has it all. A scary totem pole stands guard at the entrance. I hope it's there to protect the kids that enter. This cool park has swings, slides, teeter totters, a fire truck to climb on, and a fire pole to slide down that scares Lucy. It has a fun old-fashioned Merry-Go-Round with colorfully painted horses and bench seats.

Sometimes, I sneak a couple of quarters out of Danny's change jar so Lucy and I can go to the park and ride on the horses. Afterward, we sit along the banks of the river that snake around the park and I tell Lucy funny stories about our daddy, like when I was little and he read picture book stories to me.

"How is reading a book funny, Cart?" Lucy asks.

"Because he made stuff up that wasn't in the books," I say.

"Like what?" she asks.

"I remember one time he was reading *Goldilocks and the Three Bears.* He said the bears didn't really go out for a walk because their porridge was too hot, they went out dancing. He said there was a new dance club in town and they wanted to get their groove on, so they snuck downtown. Goldilocks saw them leave and they were all happy and frolicking so she followed them to see what was going down."

"What did she see? What do you do at a dance club?" Lucy asks.

"Goldilocks snuck inside and watched them dance, because that's what you do at a dance club, Lucy," I say with a laugh. "You dance."

"What kind of dancing?" she asks, eyes wide with excitement.

"Daddy said they liked to do the Twist because bears are kind of thick in the middle and thought it would help them thin down."

"Daddy was silly," Lucy says with a giggle. "Is the Twist a real dance? Do you know how to do it?"

I laugh out loud.

"I remember asking Daddy the same thing. Let me see if I remember. It's been a long time since he showed me."

Now, I am not one to draw attention to myself, but right there in the middle of the park, with the carousel music blasting from the Merry-Go-Round, I stand up. Along the banks of the river, I twist to the left, then twist to the right, up high and down low. The music is a little slow for the moves, but it still works.

Lucy's eyes sparkle. Her soft giggle erupts into full laughter. Next thing I know, she stands up and starts twisting next to me. She's pretty good too! People rowing by in front of us clap and cheer, and the cars driving by behind us honk their horns and wave out of their windows. I'm not sure why we aren't embarrassed, dancing like that in public, but it's been so long since we've had silly fun, we don't care. We are telling our story Daddy-style and it feels good.

8

We've been living in Freeport a month now. Danny is working extra hours at his job, still complaining that it costs too much to clothe and feed us. I'm glad he's gone more.

And for the record, I can't remember the last time we got anything new to wear, so I don't know what he's talking about. I'm sure Mama lies to him about spending the money on clothes for us, and then spends it on herself. There's hardly anything to eat around here, at least not for us. Mama says what's in the fridge is for Danny, so we end up eating a lot of peanut butter sandwiches.

Mama still doesn't do any work, although she's getting quite good at acting like the queen bee of all that is domestic. Lucy and I do the cooking, cleaning and laundry, and when Danny comes home, he's led to believe that it was Mama who did it all. He pampers her with back rubs and kindness, while harping at me and Lucy for being lazy, ungrateful brats. Why does Mama do that? Why does she let him get mad at us for not helping, knowing we're the ones who make her look good? Doesn't she see that she's making it worse for us? No wonder he doesn't want us around. For once in her life, can't she tell the truth? What kind of Mama treats her kids like this?

Today, Danny is home. It's Fourth of July. Mama and Danny have been drinking all day, so Lucy and I have been lying low. Mama says she and Danny are taking us to the fireworks show tonight. We shrug our shoulders, like it's no big deal, and play it off like it doesn't matter. They rarely follow through on anything. Secretly, we can't wait. It's been a long time since we've done anything fun. Lucy and I love the fireworks. The vibrant colors crashing to life in the dark, night sky are exciting to watch.

We spring to life when Mama calls out it's time to leave. We are really going! Danny and Mama pile us, some chairs, and a blanket into the car at dusk, and we head for the racetrack. I see Danny put a case of beer in the trunk and my spirits sink. After all of the beer they drank today, I was hoping they'd lay off of it tonight. I'm so excited to see the fireworks that I ignore it and hope for the best.

When we arrive, Mama and Danny find a good spot to set up their chairs. Lucy and I spread out the blanket in front of them to sit on. Some of their friends join the group. It's not quite dark enough for the fireworks show, but they don't care. They have their own show going on, which mostly involves drinking and being loud and obnoxious. The people around us start to notice, but again, Mama, Danny and their friends couldn't care less. I secretly hope someone will take pity on me and Lucy and whisk us away. So far, no such luck.

Across the way from where we are sitting, I catch sight of somebody who looks like Daddy. Could it be? The setting sun catches the metal of the dog tags around his neck. It makes me think of Daddy on the day he came back from Vietnam.

~

Mama and Lucy are inside taking a nap, so I sneak a Popsicle out of the freezer and sit outside on the porch steps. The hot sun melts it faster than I can eat it, so I move to the shade under the oak tree. It drips into a puddle at my feet. I drop the sticky, drippy mess in the dirt, making the ants happy. As I lick my fingers and wipe them off on my shorts, I hear whistling in the distance. I look up and see a man in a uniform walking down the sidewalk toward me. He comes closer, takes off his hat and smiles.

"Daddy, Daddy," I yell, jumping off the porch steps into his waiting arms.

I take a big sniff of him.

"Cart, baby, I have missed you," he says. "I see you're still into smelling me. I guess I still have chick magnet status."

"I can't help it, Daddy," I say. "You smell kind of different though."

"That's the military life," he says.

When I hug and sniff him again, I notice the necklace he's wearing. I pick up what looks like tags on a chain and check it out. The letters and numbers feel bumpy and raised, as I touch them.

"What's this Daddy?"

"They're my dog tags," he says.

"Dog tags?" I question. "Did you get a dog?"

I look around, excited about a new dog.

"No, baby," Daddy says with a laugh. "You get dog tags when you're in the military. It's my identification, so if I were killed or wasn't able to talk, it would tell people who I am."

He shows me his name, social security number, blood type and religion. I don't understand what it means, but I am fascinated by it just the same. I have never seen anything like this before.

Daddy and I head into the house to wake Mama and Lucy, who cries. She doesn't remember Daddy. Mama hugs him for a long time.

We spend the rest of the day at the park. Daddy lets me wear his special dog tags. Lucy warms up to Daddy in no time. It's hard not to. He chases us around in circles and we laugh and laugh as we dodge his big arms. Sometimes, we let him catch us on purpose. It feels good to have his arms around me again. Even Mama joins us and looks happy today.

That night as I lay in bed, I think about the day. I think it was my best day ever. Daddy, who I love more than anything in the world, is home again. I fall asleep squeezing his dog tags, with a smile on my face.

~

Loud laughter and disgusting belching bring me back to the racetrack. Tears cloud my vision, thinking about the possibility of that man across the way being my daddy. My heart pounds so loudly it hurts my head. I take the Magic 8 ball out of my bag and shake it. I ask it if my daddy is at the racetrack. *Better Not Tell You Now* stares back at me.

"But I want to know now!" I scream, while shaking the stupid ball. I throw it back in my bag as Mama and Danny and their friends laugh at my outburst.

"Lucy," I say quietly, ignoring their laughter. "I swear I saw Daddy."

"Are you sure?" she asks, wide-eyed, looking around. "What did the Magic 8 ball say?"

"Better Not Tell You Now."

"What should we do?" she asks.

"Let's go look for him. We can tell Mama we're going to the bathroom."

Mama barely pays attention to me as I tell her where we are going. We're not on her radar. I grab Lucy's hand and head in the direction I saw Daddy going. There are a lot of people milling about, looking for places to sit. We weave around them and find ourselves near the bathrooms.

Then, I spot him. He looks older, shaggier…different. It's been such a long time since I've seen him. Could it be him? It has to be him. He's wearing dog tags. I squeeze Lucy's hand tighter, then I break out into a run, practically dragging

51

her behind me. She cries out, trying to keep up. We reach Daddy as he turns around from the counter, beer in hand.

"Daddy?" I cry hysterically.

He is barely visible to me through the tears that are now flowing freely down my cheeks. People around us are stopping to take notice. Lucy stands frozen in fear behind me.

"Who the hell are you kid?" he replies. "I ain't your daddy."

"Is your name Jack Matthews?" I cry, wiping the snot and tears off my face.

"No, it's not. It's Paul Franks, if it's any of your business."

"Let me see your dog tags," I shout.

"Persistent little shit, aren't you?" he says.

I take a deep breath, settle down and look at him closely. He holds out his dog tags. It really isn't him. Poor Lucy. I had caused a snot fest scene for nothing.

Then, the creep says I'm kind of cute and says he'd be my daddy if I want him to be. Pervert. What in the hell is wrong with people?

Lucy and I stomp off to the laughter of creepy Paul Franks. If I ever see him again it'll be too soon.

We take our time getting back to Mama and Danny. I feel stupid for thinking that awful man could be my daddy. Lucy squeezes my hand.

"I know it's harder for you than me," Lucy says.

"I was sure it was him," I say.

"I don't remember Daddy like you do," Lucy says. "Someday, we'll find him Cart and we can get excited for real, I'm sure of it."

I squeeze Lucy's hand back. "I can't tell you how much I hope that's true."

We make it back and like I figured, no one notices we've been gone. Lucy and I sit down on the blanket hoping the fireworks hurry up and start. Mama, Danny and their friends already seem drunk. They're slurring words and laughing, acting like we don't even exist. That is until Paul Franks shows up.

"Hey, Paul," Danny yells out, staggering to stand and greet him. "June, this is Paul, I work with him at the factory."

"Nice to meet you, Pauly," Mama slurs the words and laughs. "These here are my girls."

I roll my eyes and turn away. Mama never introduces us to her friends. I hope he's too drunk to recognize me. Of all the people to know Danny.

"Where the hell are your manners, Cart?" Danny hisses out. He kicks his foot forward against my back. "Speak when spoken to for Christ's sake!"

I turn around and look up at Paul, hoping it's too dark to recognize me. No such luck.

"Hey, this here girl accused me of being her daddy over by the johns," Paul slurs out. "She was hysterical and blowing snot all over. I had to show her my dog tags. I told her I'd be her daddy if she really wants one, though."

Pedophile Paul winks down at me. He sloshes the beer out of his cup as he plops himself on the blanket next to me.

"Mama!" I scream. "Make him go away."

"What the hell, Cart?" Mama screams back. "You can't go around accusing people of being your daddy. How does that make me look?"

"Make YOU look?" I scream.

"Yeah, me," Mama hisses. "It makes me look like a tramp, you walking all over asking strange men if they're your daddy. For Christ's sake, Cart!"

"From a distance, he reminded me of my daddy," I say. "Clearly he is not. Can you please get him off of our blanket?"

As I look at Pedophile Paul, he tips over, dead drunk, his head resting on my shoulder. I try to say something to Mama and Danny, but the first fireworks shoot high into the air, lighting up the night sky with colorful splendor. No one notices me or the snoring guy on my shoulder. I blink back the burning tears.

Mama and Danny forget about us and Pedophile Paul. They're too busy oohing and aahing at the fireworks display. I jerk my shoulder away and Paul lands head first on the hard ground. I hope he has a nasty headache when he wakes up.

"Cart," Lucy says, "let's go over there on the grass and watch."

Lucy and I crawl forward and huddle together on the damp grass to watch the display. It's somehow lost its magic. Do you know that feeling of getting to do something that sounds like fun and you start out feeling super excited, only to have it end up sucking big time? And by the end of the night, there's not one thing you can come up with that makes you feel happy or glad you went? Even the fireworks you waited all night to see are ruined.

9

A couple of weeks later, Mama and Lucy walk downtown to buy Lucy a pair of shoes. I want to go too, but Mama tells me to stay home and finish the laundry. Danny's working so I don't mind having the house to myself. I'm down in the basement when I hear the aluminum door open and slam shut. I figure it's Mama and Lucy forgetting something.

As I walk up the basement steps, the hairs on my arms stand up. It's too quiet to be Mama and Lucy. I think about bolting out of the side door by the basement landing, but I want to know who's sneaking into our house. I should probably listen to my gut and leave, but I don't. Instead, I creep through the kitchen quietly and peek around the door toward the dining room.

"Looking for someone?" Danny says, stepping out from behind the door. "I heard you creeping up the steps."

I jump back and darn near wet my pants.

"You scared me. What are you doing home?"

"I live here," he says smugly, brushing my arm as he passes by me toward the kitchen.

I hear the refrigerator door open and close. If I could reach my Magic 8 Ball, it would probably tell me to run like hell and never look back. I jump when he pops the tab to his beer. I hear it hit the floor. He leaves it there and comes back into the dining room, guzzling half the beer. He belches like the pig he is and circles around me. I'm not sure why my feet don't haul it out of there. It's like they're stuck in place.

"Well, well, looks like it's just you and me, huh?" Danny says smiling that evil fake smile he has perfected. It shows up on his lips but never in his eyes, which are dead and dark.

"What are you doing home so early?" I ask, gauging my distance from the door as I slowly inch towards it.

"Again, I live here, number one," he says with great arrogance.

He takes another gulp of beer and belches. He inches closer and blows his beer belch in my face, and adds, "And number two, it's slow at work, so I'm home early."

"Mama and Lucy will be back any minute," I say, backing further away from him.

"That's funny, because I saw them walking towards downtown not two minutes ago. So, my guess is it's going to be a while before they get back. Hmm, I wonder what we can do in the meantime. There are so many options."

He inches closer, reaches out and runs his dirty fingers up and down my bare arm. I flinch at his touch. My heart sounds like a freight train. He must hear it.

"Little innocent, Cart," Danny hisses as he slowly circles around me, eyeing me like I'm the poor mouse and he is the hungry cat.

"I'm going to catch up with Mama and Lucy," I barely squeeze out, my voice cracking.

I make a move towards the door. Danny chuckles in amusement. He sets his beer down on the dining room table and spins me around. Before I know what's happening, he pins my arms above my head against the wall, pressing his body hard against mine. I swallow hard, fear clouding my brain. I want to run, but I can't budge.

As he moves his head closer, his lips crush against mine, hard and sloppy. If it wasn't for the shock, I might have thrown up in his mouth. God, please let me throw up in his mouth. I try to pull away from him, but his fingers hold my arms in place. His nails dig into my skin.

Danny reeks of beer and bad breath. I feel nauseous. His kiss is nothing like Ben's kiss, passionate and sweet. Danny's kiss makes me sick. I feel like I'm going to pass out. Dear God, please don't let me pass out. Who knows what he'll do if I'm unconscious.

He stops kissing me and looks into my eyes. "You know you want it," he says breathless, looking me up and down.

"Get the hell away from me," I scream as I fight to break free.

To shut me up, he crushes my mouth again with his. I try to bite him, but he is pushing too hard against my lips. He seems amused at my efforts to get free.

That's when I feel it in his pants, pushing against me. How am I going to get out of this? He repositions my arms together, grasping both with one hand, and with his free hand slowly reaches up the inside of my shirt. His eyes are black and a sick smile spreads across his face. He strokes my bare stomach with his fingers and begins working his way up. I struggle to get free which only seems to turn him on even more. He fumbles with my bra and then reaches underneath and touches my bare breast.

"Not as big as your mama's," he breathes heavily, "but they'll do nicely."

He stands back a bit, lifts my shirt and moves his head toward my breasts. Shock and fear give way to a fierce determination not to let him go any further. I take advantage of his distraction with my breasts and deftly swing my knee, lifting it with great force into his crotch. He jerks away from me and cries out in agony.

"You bitch!" he screams, falling to the floor, holding himself. "You are going to regret the day I ever came into your life!"

"Yeah, well I already do," I say hysterically. A wave of nausea overcomes me.

Danny lies hunched on the floor, groaning in pain. I hope it hurts like hell.

"I'm telling Mama what you did," I choke out. "She's going to leave you and take Lucy and me back to Mason."

"You aren't going to tell your Mama nothing," he says, using the table as support to lift himself up.

I back up as he gradually stands. I contemplate whether or not he'll try anything again and get my knee in position just in case. Standing, he staggers over to the table, grabs his beer and finishes it in one gulp. He limps his way to the kitchen and gets another beer. When he turns to come back into the dining room, he pauses and looks at me, a sick smile growing on his face.

"If you think I'm done with you, you are sadly mistaken," he spews out.

He pops the top to his beer, throwing the tab in my direction. He gulps the beer down.

"Next time I'll tie you down if I have to, but your ass is gonna be mine and I'm going to enjoy every minute of it."

"You won't do anything once I tell Mama," I say. "She may allow a lot of things but she would never let you hurt me like that."

"Shit, you don't know nothing about your mama," Danny says. "And like I said you're not going to tell her nothing either."

"What makes you think I won't?" I ask, crossing my arms over my chest.

"Because if you say one damn word," Danny pauses, piercing me with his dark, vengeful eyes, "I will lie and deny every word of it. I'll tell your mama you're making shit up because you hate me and are jealous of the attention she gives me. And then, when the opportunity presents itself, and trust me it will, I will go after your pain in the ass little sister. Poor little Lucy. She will be a much easier target and probably an even sweeter victory."

I gasp at his words, not able to hide my fear or disgust. He swigs the remainder of his beer and slams the empty can on the table. His threatening laugh echoes through the house. I'm too shocked to speak.

As he walks past me, he slaps my butt and gives it a little pinch, like he does to Mama.

"I've got a whole household full of bitches to keep me entertained," he says with a sickening laugh.

He jingles the car keys in his hand as he whistles his way toward the door. My tears flow freely when the aluminum door slams shut. His Firebird starts up and roars off down the street. I sit down in the chair and wail like a baby.

After I exhaust myself, I stop and wipe the snot and tears off my face with my sleeve. I pick my bag up off the floor and reach inside for my Magic 8 ball. I shake it desperately and ask it if Danny is going to molest us if we stay here. Even through my tears, I can see that it says, *Signs Point to Yes.*

"What the hell am I gonna do?" I cry. "What the hell are Lucy and I gonna do? Daddy, if you can hear me, wherever you are, please help us. Please come save us. Now."

10

I am quiet during dinner tonight. Mama doesn't notice. She never notices anything. Lucy keeps watching me though. She knows something is up. No one knows that Danny was home earlier. He hasn't come back since storming off. For all Mama knows, he's still at work.

Things have changed now. I can't get today out of my mind. What in the hell is wrong with him? Who goes after their girlfriend's daughters? What will stop him from doing it again? What if next time, he succeeds in finishing what he started out to do today? What if he goes after Lucy? I can't even think about him doing anything to Lucy. She's eleven. I will kill him. I mean, seriously kill him if he tries anything with her. Would I get sent to prison? Do they put fifteen-year-old girls in prison? Would it be considered self-defense? What if I tell Mama what he tried to do? Will she believe me or believe Danny? Will she throw me to the wolves like always? I need to think. I need to figure out a plan. Anger must be flaring up on my face because Lucy nudges me under the table, her eyes wide, curious, questioning me.

I shake my head to clear my thoughts. "So, what shoes did you get today, Lucy?" I ask, forcing a smile, hoping to lighten the mood. Lucy isn't buying it.

"Just some plain old white tennis shoes, Cart," she says. "Nothing special."

"Well, don't let Danny hear you talk like that," Mama says. "We used his hard-earned money to buy those shoes, so you better show some appreciation. It wouldn't hurt you to do something nice for him."

"We do his cooking, cleaning, and laundry already," Lucy says. "Oh, yeah, he thinks *you* do that stuff."

Mama and I both look at Lucy in surprise. She has never mouthed off to Mama. Usually, at the first sight of trouble, she either hides behind me or hides in our room.

"Aren't you getting a smart mouth like your sister," Mama says, furrowing her brow. "Cart, it would be nice if you'd stop being such a bad influence."

"Me the bad influence? Really, Mama? You bring your trashy, loser boyfriends around your innocent daughters, and I'm the bad influence? You are truly a piece of work."

I stand, pointing at Lucy, "You stay away from Danny. Do you hear me?"

Lucy looks confused. Mama's ears perk up.

"What the hell, Cart?" Mama says, standing. "Why would you say that about Danny?"

"I don't trust him," I say. "He's no good, Mama, can't you see that? We see it. What's wrong with you? He doesn't like us and I think he wants to hurt us."

"That's ridiculous," Mama says. "Danny has been nothing but wonderful to all of us. He works long, hard hours to provide for us. He's working overtime right now."

"Would you believe me if I tell you he's not what you think he is?" I ask. "Would you protect us if he's hurting us, Mama?"

"I don't know what the hell you're talking about, Cart," Mama says. "Danny doesn't like your smart mouth, if that's what you're talking about. And he's only hit you as punishment for your bad attitude."

"Ha! Whatever, Mama. You've thrown me to the wolves so many times since he's started coming around, I'm surprised I'm still alive. What if I tell you Danny is a pervert and you should leave him and take us away from here right now. Tonight. Before he gets home. Before something bad happens. Would you listen? Would you believe me?"

Recalling today's events, I know I am on the verge of getting hysterical. Lucy's face registers total fear. Mama looks genuinely confused and then, pissed.

"Cart, I am not sure what the hell is going on here," Mama says. "If you have something to say, spit it out."

"Never mind," I say, standing up to clear away the dishes. "You'd never believe me over Danny anyway. He's your free meal ticket. You're not going to screw that up. Lucy, we better get these dishes done before Danny gets home. We wouldn't want him to think Mama isn't doing her job."

"You are treading on thin ice, Cart," Mama says. She stomps off into the living room.

I pick the dishes up off the table and fill the sink with hot water and soap. Lucy is scared and confused. She sneaks off to our room. I'll talk to her later, when Mama isn't around. I wash, dry and put away the dishes. I'm ok with not having Lucy to help me. It gives me time to think. I hoped Mama would come into the kitchen to help and maybe ask me what's going on. My heart lurches when she does walk into the kitchen, but she grabs a beer from the fridge and never looks my way.

When your daughter tells you she thinks your boyfriend is a pervert, don't you think you'd be smart enough to ask a few questions? Does she only care about herself? Does she care if her sleazy boyfriend is trying to have sex with me? If I march into the living room and tell her everything that happened today, will she believe me? Will she call me a liar?

After I clean up the kitchen, I walk through the dining room to go upstairs. Mama is on the couch flipping through a magazine and drinking a beer. She doesn't bother to look up or say good night. Aren't mamas supposed to tell you good night, I love you, sweet dreams and all that good stuff? Mama never says those things to me. My daddy used to say them every night. He'd tuck me in and make me feel safe and loved. Mama never picked up where he left off. It's been nothing but emptiness since he left.

I sneak into our room, closing the door behind me. I move the chair in front of it and make sure it's lodged good and tight underneath the door knob. I don't bother to turn on the light.

"What's going on, Cart?" Lucy asks. "Something happened. I can tell."

"You should be sleeping," I say, avoiding her question. It comes out harsher than I intend.

"I can't sleep," she says. "I can see you are scared and that scares me. Are we in trouble? What happened?"

The glow of the streetlight streaming through the window shows me the worry and fear in her eyes. I don't answer her. Instead, I get ready for bed. There are so many things swirling around in my head. I'm not sure what to tell her. I don't want to scare her, but at the same time, I want her to know we are no longer safe here. I climb into bed. Lucy rolls over as far away from me as she can without falling out. I can tell she's crying but doesn't want me to know.

"Lucy," I say, pulling on her shoulder. She turns to face me. "Danny came home today while you and Mama were downtown getting shoes. He got off work early. He was drinking beer and being his normal jerky self, but then, he changed. He tried to, you know, make a move on me. Kiss me."

I can't bring myself to tell Lucy everything. Or that he threatened to do the same to her. It would scare her. I want her to be careful around him and never be alone with him, but I don't want to freak her out. I don't know what she knows about sex. Probably not much because I haven't told her anything and Mama's too busy participating in it to tell her anything. Neither of us should ever have to worry about our Mama's boyfriends wanting to molest us.

"Where is he now?" she asks.

"I don't know," I answer. "He left after I kicked him in the crotch and he hasn't come back. Mama thinks he's still at work. I'd like to think he slithered off and died, but he's probably out drinking. We need to be careful."

"You kicked him in the crotch?" she asks.

"Yeah, with my knee." I giggle a bit, remembering the stunned and pained look on his stupid face. I wanted to kick him over and over in the crotch until it either fell off, or he promised to leave and never come back. Or died. That would have been ok, too.

"That had to make him really mad, Cart," she says. "Is he coming back or is he gone for good?"

"I don't know. He's probably coming back. God, he was mad. Real mad. But, I'd do it again if I had to," I say. "It dropped him right to the floor. Remember that, if you're ever in a crappy situation. Guys don't like getting kicked there. It hurts like hell. Aim well and kick hard. And if given the opportunity, keep doing it until they scream mercy or until they stop moving."

"How did you know that would hurt him?"

"Back when we lived in Mason, I was dusting Mama's room and saw a pamphlet on self-defense for women. So, I read it. I think that was around the time of George. You probably don't remember him. He yelled a lot and Mama ended up with a lot of bruises. He didn't stick around too long."

"Maybe it's not such a bad thing that we have to dust Mama's room," Lucy says. "It seems to be a good way to find out about life-saving stuff."

I laugh. "You have a point there! And what's with sassing Mama tonight? You never do that."

64

"I don't know, Cart," Lucy says, just as surprised. "It escaped my mouth before I realized I said it out loud. I think all of the same things you do; only, I never say them out loud. I was scared, though. I thought Mama was going to slap me."

"I thought she was too," I say. "We're going to have to be more careful. Things are changing. Mama is worse now than she's ever been. I thought for sure Danny would have hit the road by now. Mama never sticks with them for too long. So far, I think he's the longest. We need to make sure we take extra care of each other until he gets the boot. We need to make sure we are never put in a position where we are alone with him. And I mean never. Do you understand that, Lucy? If it happens, leave. Run out of the house and stay with a neighbor or hide until someone else comes home."

"Ok, Cart," Lucy says.

"I'm not trying to scare you," I say. "But you have to be smart. If you get an icky vibe, listen to it."

"Ok, I will," Lucy says.

I hug Lucy and kiss the top of her head. Soon, her breathing becomes slow and rhythmic. She's asleep. As I try to drift off too, that familiar knot begins forming in my stomach. I know Danny will come back. I'm not sure what's going to happen though. Will Mama tell Danny what I said? Will he lie and deny and wait for a chance to hurt me and Lucy? I can't get out my Magic 8 Ball. I'm too afraid of what it's going to say. Somehow, I think I already know the answer.

I wake up sometime later when I hear the front door. I lie perfectly still, straining my ears for any sound at all. At first, there are soft voices talking and then, they get louder. I hear lots of swearing and the sound of something being thrown.

Then it's quiet, too quiet. I swallow hard when I hear footsteps on the stairs. They stop outside of our door. I hear weeping. Mama. The doorknob jiggles, but she's not able to get in, so she moves on to her bedroom.

Another set of footsteps climb the stairs. Danny. I hold my breath. If that door doesn't hold, I don't know what I'm going to do. I jump when I hear his hand smack against the wall next to our door. He mumbles something. I don't hear him walk away. Is he standing outside our door? Is he going to try and get in here? Mama must have said something to him. Why didn't I just shut up and not say anything? I rack my brains, trying to remember everything I said.

Sometimes, when you're mad, stuff spews from your mouth and you don't remember half of it. I can't recall saying anything other than he's a pervert. She has to have figured *that* out by now. I jump when I hear another smack on the wall. Danny mumbles again, and then I hear him stomp down the hall. The door to their bedroom slams shut. Then, it gets quiet.

11

The next morning, the sun peeks into our bedroom window and wakes me with a start. I gaze down at Lucy, glad she's still snuggled next to me. I attempt to smooth her wild hair with my hand. Her face looks crumpled with worry and sadness, even while she sleeps. I glance over at the door. The chair is exactly where I left it last night.

I listen for any movement in the house. Nothing. Do we hide out in here all day? Do we get dressed, sneak downstairs and hang out in the park? Do we face the music and see what happens? I hate the unknown. I hate surprises. I hate worry and fear. I hate Danny.

I reach over the side of the bed for my Magic 8 ball and ask it if things are going to change. *As I See It, Yes.* Before I have a chance to think about whether that's good or bad, Lucy stirs next to me and stretches herself awake.

"Cart?" Lucy says, "I'm hungry. Will you go downstairs with me? I don't want to go alone. I heard Danny come home last night."

"You heard him?" I ask. "I thought you were asleep."

"I heard them fighting. What are we going to do?"

I take a deep breath.

"I don't know." I say after a few minutes, "Let's pack our school backpacks with clothes and things we might need if we have to leave in a hurry."

"Leave?" Lucy says. "Where would we go? Are we going to run away? And leave Mama?"

"I'm not saying we are and I'm not saying we're not," I say. "We just need to be prepared for anything. I have no clue what we're going to face once we move the chair away from the door and walk out of this room."

Tears fall down Lucy's face.

"Don't cry," I say, wiping her tears with my hand. "I've been trying to remember and I think Daddy said his mama, our grandma, lives in Freeport. I'm almost sure of it. When we first came here, the name Freeport sounded familiar to me. If it gets crappy, maybe we can try and find her."

"Grandma?" Lucy says. "Didn't you tell me Daddy said she was mean? I don't want to live with someone who's mean."

"I know, Lucy," I reassure, "but Danny went from being stupid to creepy, and that is worse than mean."

"You mean him kissing you?" she asks.

"Yeah," I say.

I pause, gauging how much to reveal.

"Lucy, Danny was pushing to go a lot farther than kissing. Do you understand what I'm saying?"

"You mean sex?" she whispers. "Our teacher talks about sex and periods in our health class. It's gross, Cart. I want to talk to you about it, but it's embarrassing. I can't believe people actually do that stuff…and like it. And periods, once a month? Is that some kind of sick joke?"

I have to giggle. I've had my period since I was twelve. Sick joke is right! Of course, when I got it, Mama didn't tell me anything. When I told her I got it, she acted all weird and told me it was part of life and now I better steer clear of the boys. She gave me some of her tampons, but I had to figure out how to use them. I guess she gets the Mother of the Year

Award for doing half of a motherly thing. Every month, she gives me money to buy tampons for us both. She won't go get them. Do you know how embarrassing it is to stand in the check-out line with tampons in your hand while boys you know from school walk in and see you?

"Cart," Lucy says, pushing on my arm. "Can we talk about all of this stuff?"

"Later," I promise, "but you need to know that it's wrong, very wrong, for Danny to try and do any of that stuff with us. Or any other kid, for that matter! We have to make sure we are smart and never get put in that situation. Make sure you are never alone with him anywhere...especially at home."

"You don't have to tell me twice," Lucy says.

Lucy hugs me and I hug her back. We are a team. I love her so much. The best thing Mama and Daddy ever did was make Lucy. I know she feels the same way about me. I can't help but think if we stick together, we'll be ok. At least I hope so. We can *never* be separated.

We get out of bed and get dressed for the day. Digging our backpacks out of the closet, we fill them with clothes and underwear. I help Lucy brush her hair and braid it into pig tails. I brush mine back into a ponytail and shove the hairbrush, along with a thin blanket from my bed, into the bag with my Magic 8 Ball. I figure we can throw our toothbrushes in later, along with some food from the kitchen, if that's what it comes down to us having to do. I hope not. I hope we're just being overly cautious. I don't want to have to find Daddy's mama. I want to walk downstairs and find my own mama waiting for us, telling us everything will be ok; that we're going back to Mason. That she knows Danny is a jerk and she loves us more than him. I want to hear her say she's sorry, she's going to be a better Mama now that she has seen the light and realizes we're more important than any guy.

Lucy and I shove our backpacks under the bed so no one will see them. We move the chair away from the door, turn the doorknob and head out to see if our lives are going to change.

12

I peek my head out of the door, look toward the bathroom and then down the hall toward *their* bedroom. Lucy is glued to my back like a Siamese twin. I don't see or hear anyone. Maybe they're still sleeping or gone.

We make our way down the stairs, careful to avoid the loud, squeaky steps. We know which ones to dodge. We have escaped many confrontations by staying invisible. It's hard not to feel like little mice avoiding the big, bad hungry cats.

Once at the bottom of the stairs, I stick my head into the living room. No one there. I turn toward the dining room. Empty. Usually, they're either in the living room, dining room or their bedroom. Neither one knows what to do in a kitchen. It looks like the coast is clear. Feeling confident, our stomachs lead us to the kitchen for food.

"How's peanut butter toast sound?" I ask Lucy.

"Really good," she answers. "I'm hungry."

As we round the corner to the kitchen, Mama and Danny are sitting at the table. Shit. Double shit. I freeze in place. Lucy gasps, running behind me faster than a turtle taking cover in its shell. They *never* sit in the kitchen. That's the spot they've designated for us. They only sit in the dining room. The knot in my stomach burns double time. Before we can haul it out of there, both Mama and Danny turn to face us.

"You're up," Mama says. "Danny and I need to talk to you."

For once, I have nothing to say. I stand there. I have no clue what either of them are going to say or how it'll come out for us in the end. What does she mean Danny and I need to talk to you? That implies some sort of an alliance. The fact that they're sitting there together, must mean something. Why do I hear the wolves howling?

"Danny and I had a long conversation last night," she begins. "He told me he came home early from work yesterday. He said you were in a crappy mood and you threatened to tell me he tried to molest you. Quite frankly, Cart, I'm a little disappointed in you for resorting to such horrible lies to break us up. He said he left as soon as he realized you and he were the only ones home and there were no witnesses to confirm your lies. He went to Tommy's house and decided to stay away longer so that we could have some time together without him. He thought that must be what you are missing, and why you lied."

Whoa. Did Danny ever do a number on Mama. Her back is to him and she can't see the sickening grin on his face growing wider by the minute. If only I could projectile puke. Of course, he looks serious and concerned when she turns to look back at him. At this point, I'm not sure what to say. The jerk did exactly what he said he would do. I should have told her everything last night before he had a chance to lie.

"What do you have to say for yourself?" Mama asks.

"He's a pervert, he's lying and he *did* try to molest me and threatened to hurt Lucy. Ask him how his crotch feels today. He got my big, bony knee right square in the middle of it. He could hardly walk out of here when he left. Bet you didn't have sex last night, did you Mama? Can't you see what's going on? Get us out of here. Let's go back to Mason.

For once, can't you put us first instead of yourself and your sleazy boyfriends?"

I begin crying, which is something I never do in front of anyone. Mama has to see that means I'm telling the truth.

"Forever the drama queen," Mama says to me. "I should enroll you in acting classes."

I glare at them through my tears. In the end, she thinks I'm crying because she caught me in a lie. What a load. I never, in a million years, would have imagined what she was going to say next.

"I want you to be the first to know that Danny has asked me to marry him," Mama says. "We're going out to look at rings today."

"Marry you?" I cry. "Are you kidding me? Do you even know who this man is, Mama? He forced himself on me yesterday. He covered my mouth in his slobbery, stinky kisses. He reached under my shirt and bra. He threatened to tie me down to get what he wants. He pushed himself all over me," I cry, pointing at his privates.

Mama stands and slaps my face. She's looking at me like I'm some sort of monster. "Stop lying, Cart," Mama says. "Danny would *never* do anything like that."

"And you, Mama," I scream. "You are the queen of lying. You don't do shit around this house. Lucy and I do it all. Tell Danny what a lazy person you are. Tell Danny that it's Lucy and me who do the cooking, cleaning and laundry, while you lay on the couch reading your magazines and drinking your beer. Tell Danny you couldn't boil water if your sorry ass depended on it. Tell him you have no idea how to run the washer and dryer and probably don't even know which one is which. Tell Danny it's us who cleaned this filthy house the day we moved in and have done so every day since."

"McCartney Matthews," Danny says, standing up, kicking his chair back. "Your Mama has done nothing but work her ass off around here and take care of you ungrateful kids. You tell her you're sorry."

"Hell, no!" I scream.

Danny starts huffing towards me but Mama stops him.

"Now, Cart," she says, not addressing the whole doing nothing issue, because she knows damn well she's in the wrong and is lying straight through her teeth. "You need to start listening to Danny. We've talked about it. He wants to adopt you and Lucy. He wants to be your daddy."

I feel like I've been sucker punched in the gut. Lucy is crying behind me. Danny stands behind Mama, that ugly, creepy smile filling his face.

"You'll get used to calling me Daddy," Danny says. "In no time at all, you'll grow to like it. I know you and Lucy both will grow to like it."

At this point, I'm not sure if he's talking about calling him Daddy or talking about something else.

"I will *never* call you daddy," I say. "And if you *ever* come near me or Lucy, I will kill you. I will leave your stinking, rotting body on the stoop out front as a sign to any and all other future boyfriends that Lucy and I are off limits and this is what happens if you think otherwise."

"McCartney Matthews, that is enough," Mama says.

Danny smiles that cold, insincere smile that never reaches his eyes.

"They need to think about everything we laid on them, baby," he says. "We'll go run those errands so they can let it soak in. We will be a very close-knit new family."

As Mama and Danny leave the kitchen, he looks at Lucy and me and winks. We both stand there dumbfounded. I know right then and there we are screwed. I know what Danny is referring to and it has nothing to do with being our daddy. I also know Mama will never protect us. We have no choice. We have to leave.

13

The sound of Danny's car speeding away puts my brain into high gear. Lucy comes out from behind me sobbing uncontrollably.

"What are we going to do, Cart?"

"We are *not* staying here," I say, letting anger replace the fear, now that he's gone.

"Where will we go? I don't want to find the mean Grandma," she says, hugging her arms around my waist.

"I don't know. We need money," I say. "Help me grab some food, and we'll put it with our stuff upstairs."

Lucy and I move quickly through the kitchen and gather up peanut butter, bread, a few apples and a couple of spoons.

Once in our room, I tell her to pack the food in our bags while I sneak off to Mama and Danny's room. I need to move fast in case they come back. I go to Danny's dresser first. A dish of change along with a hairbrush sits on top. Pretty sure that hairbrush hasn't seen a follicle of his greasy hair since he purchased it. What a pig! I dump the change into my pocket. I open the top drawer and start rummaging through his underwear. There is nothing more disgusting than picking through the underwear drawer of someone you hate the most in this world. As I dig deeper toward the back, my hand hits something hard. A box. I pull it out and look it over. It's not too big, about the size of my transistor radio, and it's locked. There must be something important in it for him to keep it locked away and hidden in his underwear drawer. The sound of Danny's car coming back makes me jump. Maybe that car isn't so bad after all. It gives me fair warning.

"They're coming back, Cart," Lucy yells from her bedroom. "What do we do? Do we hide? Or act like nothing's going on? I'm scared, Cart."

I take the locked box and bring it back with me to our bedroom.

"All I could find was this," I say, holding out the box. "Now that they're coming back, we don't have time to break into it. We're going to have to take it with us but we have to go now. If it has money in it, we need it. And I don't feel guilty taking it. Consider it payment for him being a creepy jerk."

I shove the box into my backpack as the car turns onto our street. I hear it getting closer.

"Lucy, we have to go *now*," I say, the urgency in my voice causes her to cry. "No crying! We're going to be ok. Did you put the food in our backpacks?"

"Yes," she says, sobbing. "Some in yours and some in mine."

"Ok, good. We're going to run down these steps as fast as we can, through the dining room and into the kitchen. Head to the side door on the basement landing. We'll sneak out there and make our way down the alley, staying close to the garages. Understand?"

"Yes," Lucy says, slinging her backpack over her shoulder.

I do the same and we make a mad dash for the stairs. We hear Danny's car pull up and shut off, followed by a door slamming shut as we race down the steps. My heart pounds so hard, it throbs in my head and blurs my vision. We can't get caught leaving, especially with Danny's stuff on us. We round the corner into the dining room as the front door opens. We make it into the kitchen and unlatch the basement door as Danny runs up the steps to his bedroom. Is he looking for us? Did he forget something? What are the odds he wants what's in the box we stole? As I open the side door and we sneak out, I hear him yelling and stomping through the rooms upstairs.

"Where's my box you little bitches? Where are you? I'm going to beat you both for stealing my stuff!"

Lucy and I run through the backyard and down the alley like our lives depend on it. I don't know what's in the box, but it's clearly something Danny wants. And now we have it.

Chills run through my body despite the hot, August day. There's no going back now. Danny will probably beat us…or worse, if we're caught. Maybe he'll call the cops because we stole from him. He's already proven he's a successful liar. He'll have the cops on his side in no time.

We are officially on our own. Homeless. I should be scared, but right now, I'm more afraid of getting caught by Danny. There must be something valuable in that box. I'm glad we have it. This sort of adrenaline rush is powerful enough to kill a person.

"I'm scared, Cart," Lucy cries, as we run down the alley. "I need to catch my breath."

"We need to get as far away from here as we can," I say. "Can't you go a little farther?"

"No," Lucy says. Tears run down her face. I can see she is heading for a breakdown.

"Ok," I say. "We'll hide out between the two garages up ahead, but just long enough to make a plan."

Lucy and I slow down as we approach the garages at the end of the alley. There is barely enough space to sneak between the broken fencing blocking the passage between the two buildings. I try not to think about the creatures that could be living here. The last thing I want to do is scream and let on we're here.

We get inside, just as we hear Danny's car pull into the alley. He is driving slowly. I'm so nervous, I feel like I could pee. We crouch down among the weeds and brush, hoping to disappear from sight. The rumbling of his car is close. Too close. I lift my head and see them right in front of us. Mama's window is down. They are both looking out of the window on Danny's side. Mama turns her head toward her own window. I quickly lay back down, grateful for the coverage.

"Are you sure they came this way?" Danny asks Mama as they slow to a stop in front of the garages.

"Yes, I saw them run out of the side door with their backpacks and head down the alley," she answers.

"Why didn't you stop them?"

"How the hell was I supposed to know what they were doing? It's not unlike them to come in and out of the side door. I had no clue they stole your box."

Mama looks in our direction and we lean even farther back, lying completely flat on the ground. We hold our breath, hoping the weeds are tall enough to hide us. If they aren't, it's all over for us. Lucy starts to whimper. I squeeze her arm. She stops and lies perfectly still.

"They couldn't have gotten far," Danny says. "When I catch them, they are going to be sorry. Nobody steals from me and walks away from it."

"Maybe you misplaced the box," Mama says. "We can clear this up when they get home."

"There's nothing to clear up," Danny says. "They stole it and when I find them, they are going to pay."

"They're just children," Mama says.

Could Mama be defending us? Is there hope that Mama would help us?

"June," Danny says. "There was money in that box and that's what I was going to buy your ring with. No money. No ring. I worked my ass off for that money."

"Those little shits," Mama says. "I knew that Cart would be a bad influence on Lucy and now Lucy's just as bad as she is. They're going to have to be punished."

So much for Mama helping us.

"I don't see them," Danny says. "Let's drive around town to the places they like to go. If we don't see them, we'll head to the bar. I need a drink. Eventually, they'll come back and get what they deserve."

"Oh, yes they will," Mama chimes in.

Finally, they move down the alley. I want to cry like a baby, but can't do that to Lucy. I need to stay strong for her. Where can we go and how can we stay hidden from Danny and Mama? What if they go to the police and they start looking for us too? We have nowhere to go, no one to trust and everyone to fear. Oh, Daddy, where are you?

14

Lucy and I sit up and look at each other. I swear I can hear her heart pounding. She can probably hear mine, too.

"What does your Magic 8 Ball say?" she asks.

I reach into my bag and take it out. I give it a good, solid shake. With a trembling voice, I ask it, "Will Lucy and I be ok?"

I stop shaking the ball.

Concentrate And Ask Again.

I sigh, take a deep breath, shake the Magic 8 Ball and ask, "Will Danny find us and hurt us?"

I stop shaking the ball.

Signs Point to Yes.

I put the Magic 8 Ball back into my bag, avoiding eye contact with Lucy. She doesn't say a word. We stand up and brush the dirt off of our clothes. She sees the stress on my face. I try to hide it but am just as scared as she is.

"Cart," Lucy says in a whisper. "What are we going to do? I don't want Danny to catch us, but how long can we stay away? We don't know how to be homeless. He's going to find us. I'm afraid. Can't we just sneak the box back into his drawer and tell him maybe it got moved when we put laundry away or something? Then, he won't be mad and we'll be safe."

"Lucy, even if we put the box back and act like we didn't do anything, we're not safe. Danny is out to get us. We'll never be safe around him. He went after me and I will never allow him to go after you. We have to leave."

"What if he catches us?" Lucy begins crying again.

I put my brave face on and grab Lucy by the shoulders and make her look me right in the eyes.

"We can stay hidden until we figure out a plan. Maybe we can go back to Mason. They won't look for us there. There's a bus station downtown. Maybe we can get tickets and take a bus back. And if push comes to shove, we'll go to the cops and tell them everything."

"What if they don't believe us and send us right back to Mama and Danny? I'd rather go to Mason," Lucy says, her tone and eyes brightening. "We know people in Mason, but we need money to get there."

"Money," I say. "Yes, money."

I reach into my bag for Danny's box. I look it over in my hand, turning it around to check out the lock. It's cheap, thin and old, just like Danny.

"Do you have a bobby pin?" I ask Lucy.

She fishes around the hair on the back of her head. After a minute, smiles as she pulls one out.

I laugh as she hands it to me.

"What else do you have in there?" I ask.

"Not much, but you never know," Lucy says with a smile. "When I put my hair in a high ponytail, I use bobby pins in the back to help hold my hair up. Sometimes, I don't find them all."

"Your hair is like a small rat's nest," I say.

"Lucky for us," she responds.

I agree, as I put the bobby pin to my mouth and chew off the protective plastic, rubbery piece that keeps them from poking into your head. I spit the plastic piece out on the ground, as I jimmy the pin into the lock, twisting it.

"How do you know this stuff?" Lucy asks.

"I've been watching Mama a long time," I say. "I think I've learned a new trick with each new boyfriend she's brought home. I learned this one when Joe was in the picture. I liked to call him Lumberjack Joe. Big, hairy fella, about as bright as a burned out light bulb. I think he was the nicest one out of all of them. He used to bring me candy and he never yelled. He kept his money hidden similar to this and Mama would find it, break into it and take a few quarters here and a dollar there. It took him a while to put two and two together and when he finally did, he moved on."

"Mama sure has a goofy way of teaching us stuff, huh, Cart?" Lucy says. "Is that bobby pin working yet?"

"Not so far," I say. "I've done this a million times on the lock in the bathroom when you're taking too long, but never on this kind of lock before."

"Yeah, I am aware of that," Lucy says.

"It's not my fault you take so long."

"Sometimes, it's just nice to have a quiet place to relax," Lucy says.

"I don't think *that's* going to be possible anymore now that Danny's around," I say. "Maybe, once we get this open and get tickets to Mason, we can look up my friend Ben. I bet he'll be able to help us."

"Ben?" Lucy asks. "Who's Ben and how come I don't know anything about him?"

A smile creeps across my face. "He's a boy I know back in Mason. He was in my class. On the last day of school, he pulled me into the apple grove near our house and kissed me. I ran like an idiot after he did it and then, the next day we moved."

"He kissed you?" Lucy asks. "Did you like it?"

"Maybe," I say, that smile now bursting across my face.

Lucy smiles. *"Cart and Ben sitting in a tree. K-I-S-S-I-N-G. First comes love, then comes marriage, then comes a baby in a baby carriage."*

"Very funny," I say, not able to hide my cheesy smile.

I twist and turn the bobby pin in the lock a few more times and it clicks open. Lucy and I high five.

"It's open," she says.

"Now, let's see what's in here," I answer. "If he was going to buy Mama a wedding ring, we should be able to get pretty far and be good for a while."

I pull the lock off and throw it in weeds. I lift up the metal flap and open the lid.

"Wow," I say, fishing out a wad of bills, rubber banded together.

I hand the box to Lucy.

"I don't want to get caught with this," she says.

She throws it in the weeds with the lock. I pull the rubber band off the bills and unfold the wad. Leafing through them, it looks like a bunch of one, five and ten-dollar bills. I count the stack.

"Seventy-five dollars," I say. "Some wedding ring he's going to get with that. I don't know why Mama believes the crap that comes from his mouth. He is no more going to buy her a wedding ring than he's going to make a good husband. Or daddy for that matter. God help us if they have a child together."

"So, what do we do now?" Lucy asks.

"Let's take the side streets to downtown and see if we can get bus tickets. We need to stay hidden from Danny. It's a good thing we can hear his car coming from a mile away. We also need to hide from the cops, in case Danny went to them and reported us."

"Can we get arrested for taking his money?" Lucy asks.

"I don't know. Maybe not once I tell them what Danny tried to do," I say, "if they believe me."

"I hope they believe you," she says. "I believe you."

I smile as I shove the wad of bills into my backpack. We walk to the edge of the garages and peek out. I look up the alley toward our house and then, down the street by the school. No car. No Danny. As long as he stays in the car to look for us, we'll have the advantage. If he looks for us on foot, we won't hear him coming. I wonder if he'll tell his friends to keep an eye out for us. If he does that, I don't know what we'll do. We won't know who to watch out for. We need to get to Mason as soon as we can.

Lucy and I avoid all of the well-traveled streets as we make our way downtown. Every time we hear a loud car, we crouch down behind a parked vehicle until it passes. I'm hoping by now, Danny and Mama are well established on a bar stool somewhere, forgetting about Lucy and me, like they usually do.

Finally, we make it to the bus station. A big greyhound dog looks like it's leaping across the sign on the wall above the door. Lucy and I stick close together. No one seems to pay attention to us and we don't see any cops. That's a good sign. We walk up, pull open the heavy door and step inside. It's just as hot inside as it is outside. We see plastic chairs lined in rows with a few vending machines against the dirty cinder block walls. It's not cheery or pleasant. We walk up to the ticket counter.

"I'd like two tickets to Mason," I say to the man behind the tall bar-lined window.

He eyes me up and down with disapproval.

"You and this one here traveling alone, Missy?" he asks, pointing to Lucy, who takes a step backward and moves behind me.

"Our Mama is next door at the laundromat changing out the clothes," I say in a sweet voice, using my best smile. "She told us to come get our tickets. We're going to spend some time in Mason with our Grandma. Mama is going to wait outside with us until our bus comes. We moved here a few months ago from Mason and haven't seen our Grandma since we left."

"Is that so?" The old man says.

"Yes, sir," I respond with a smile. "It'll be good to see her again."

"You seem to be on the up and up," he says. "Can't tell you how many kids come through here trying to run away. I can usually pick 'em out pretty good, so I don't sell 'em tickets."

Lucy inches a little farther behind me and I continue smiling. "How much are the tickets, Sir?"

"Six dollars each," he says. "One way."

I reach into my backpack for $12 and place it on the counter.

"Our grandma's going to buy our return tickets," I say. "We're not sure how long we'll be there."

The man takes our money and holds out the tickets. I reach up for them and smile sweetly.

"Bus number five thirty will be out front in fifteen minutes."

"Thank you," I say.

Feeling triumphant, I place the tickets in my backpack and grab Lucy's hand, turning towards the door. I stop dead in my tracks and gasp. My legs give out and I balance myself on Lucy. I can't catch my breath. Every ounce of satisfaction I was feeling went straight down the shitter.

"Hello, girls," Danny says, standing inside the door, his arms crossed.

I turn to the old man, who looks up. I'm sure to him the smile on Danny's face looks genuine. I can see that Danny is beyond pissed off. His eyes are near black.

15

"Thank you, sir," Danny says, with a sweet, convincing smile, to the old man behind the counter. "Their Mama and I will wait outside with them until their bus comes. They sure have been looking forward to seeing their grandma."

Apparently, he had been listening long enough to hear my lie. He smiles that dangerous smile that never quite reaches his eyes, which are, at this moment, growing darker by the second. My blood freezes. Lucy burrows into my back.

"You all have a great day," the old man says. "It's good to see such caring parents."

"We do our best," Danny says. "These girls mean everything to their Mama and me."

Danny walks towards us. He reaches out and grabs my wrist and pulls me toward him. Then, he grabs Lucy's wrist. I wince at the pressure he applies. Lucy whimpers. We walk toward the door.

"Open the door," he says to me, squeezing my wrist harder.

I do as he says. Do I look back at the old man and hope he sees the fear on my face? If I do, then what happens? Danny has Lucy separated from me. I can't break free and run. I wouldn't be able to grab Lucy fast enough. I'll take whatever Danny has to dish out before I'll leave Lucy.

Any opportunity to have the old man help is gone once we step outside. Danny drags us to the side of the building, out of the man's sight. No one is around except for Mama, who is waiting in the car. She gets out and walks up to us. She slaps my face and grabs my backpack. She digs inside for the wad of money, takes it, and then shoves the backpack into my chest. I grab it with my free hand. Danny is still squeezing the hell out of our wrists. Lucy has gone from whimpering to deep sobbing. Danny lets go of Lucy and shoves her toward Mama. He still has the death grip on me. Mama grabs Lucy, opens the car door, and pushes the seat forward.

"Get in," she says, motioning toward the backseat. "I'm very disappointed in you."

"Me? What about you? Cart's not lying, Mama," Lucy says, as Mama shoves her into the back.

"I would expect no less from you, lying for your sister," she says. "You're just like her."

"Good," Lucy says. "She's the best thing that has ever happened to me."

Mama throws the front seat back and gets in and sits down. She slams the door shut and looks out of the window.

"You both will be punished," Mama says to Lucy. "Don't forget who calls the shots."

Lucy doesn't respond but I can see her watching what Danny is doing with me.

He walks me over to the driver door, but before he opens it, he pulls me in closely and whispers so that no one can hear him. "Sweet, Sweet, Cart," he says. "It will be a joy to punish you and your sister for stealing my money and causing your mama such hardship. I will have to think long and hard about what you deserve."

He squeezes my arm tighter. I look into his eyes and swear I can see straight into his dead, black soul. He opens the door, pulls the front seat forward and pushes me into the back. He pinches my butt as I bend forward to get inside. I can't blink back the tears nor hide them from Lucy. I'm scared. I feel horrible when I see the pain on her face. What the hell kind of sister am I? Maybe if I had learned to keep my big mouth shut, we wouldn't be in this situation. I have failed Lucy. I don't deserve her in my life.

Danny whistles as he pushes his seat back and gets in. He starts up the engine and pulls up to the edge of the street. Bus five thirty has just rolled in. I can't believe we missed freedom by fifteen minutes. Fifteen flipping minutes!

Lucy and I sit in silence in the back seat. I'm not sure what to do. I need to think. We can't stay with them. It's clear we won't be safe. Danny won't stop until he gets what he wants. Mama has blinders on and only sees a free meal ticket. I don't know how to make her see that Danny is a sick jerk. Will it take her catching him raping me and Lucy before she gets it? Even then, will she think it's our fault, or that we seduced him? Is she stupid enough to believe that?

Don't you sometimes wonder what you're put on this earth to accomplish? Why do we get the family and life that we do? What are we supposed to get out of it all? How do we figure out how to survive?

About the only thing I *do* know for sure is that I am not here for myself, but for Lucy, to protect her, love her and help her grow up as happy as I can. I want her to know that someone on this earth loves her. Me. If I do that well, I don't need anything else. Except for maybe to find my daddy and let *him* know he is loved. His Mama sucked at showing him love and so did my Mama. Maybe if he knows someone really loves him, he'll come back. He deserves to be loved.

Why did God choose Mama for me? Maybe she was given to me as an example of how not to be towards any children I may have. And Danny? Maybe he's here to show me how to protect myself and Lucy and learn to be strong and independent. What a crappy way to have to learn that.

I hope one day my reward in this life will be to sit with my daddy while we listen to Beatles music. I want to giggle as I watch the Beatles bobbleheads nod to the music. I want to sit so close to my daddy, that I can smell him, and know it's him, even if my eyes are closed. I want to have peace in my soul and the hole that has grown so large in my heart to be healed.

The other day I heard the Beatle's song 'Blackbird' on my transistor radio. I cried as I listened to the lyrics. I'm not sure what the words are supposed to mean, but for me, they give me hope. One day I'm going to fly above this crappy life I've been given and be free. I hope my daddy will be a part of that. But if he's not, Lucy and I will make it. I have to believe that. We might be throw away sisters, but we're survivors.

16

Far too quickly, we arrive at Float Street. Nobody has said a word since leaving the bus station. Danny is blasting a Lynyrd Skynyrd 8 track. *Free Bird* keeps playing over and over. If he wants to be free, I will be first in line to show him the door. I hope it slams him square and fair on his sorry behind as he's pushed out.

Lucy reaches over and holds my hand. I squeeze hers back to let her know it's going to be ok. Somehow it's going to be ok. I *will* make our broken wings fly. Danny pulls up in front of the house and shuts off the engine. The sudden quiet is deafening and awkward. We sit in complete silence. Mama is the first to speak.

"Go to your room," she says to Lucy and I. "Danny and I need to talk. We will be up in a little while."

Mama opens her door and steps out of the car. Danny follows suit. They both push their seats forward so we can get out of the back. Lucy and I squeeze each other's hand before we let go. We grab our backpacks and exit the car. Mama lets Lucy walk by her without a word. Danny grins and pinches my arm as I pass him. I try not to make eye contact with him. I won't give him the satisfaction of seeing the fear in my eyes. Lucy and I meet up on the other side and walk up to the house. We open the door and step inside. It slams shut behind us. Danny swears. I want to rip that door off its hinges.

As we turn toward the stairs, for a brief moment, I think about walking from the front door straight out the back door and running like hell. Since it didn't work out so great the first time we tried it, I decide not to do it. Besides, Mama took the money. We need a new plan. Once safely in our room, with the chair wedged in front of the door, we crawl into bed and break down and cry.

"I'm sorry, Lucy," I say, sitting up. I look down at my mood ring. I stare into its dark emptiness.

"Sorry for what?" she asks. "Without you, I would be worse off."

"I'm not sure about that," I say.

"We need to stick together, no matter what," Lucy says. "We'll be ok, as long as we stay together."

"When did you get so grown up and smart?" I ask, giving her a long hug.

"I've had a great teacher," she says. "I'm hungry."

"Me too," I say, "but I'm not going down there."

"Me either," she says. She jumps off the bed and grabs her backpack. "I packed food. We can stay up here for a few days, at least."

We enjoy a great snack of peanut butter bread and an apple, and pack the leftovers safely away, just in case.

"What do you think they're going to do?" Lucy asks.

"I don't know. I don't want to think about it."

"When do you think they'll come up?" she asks.

"I hope never."

I reach for my backpack and pull out the Magic 8 Ball and give it a good shake.

"Is the punishment Mama and Danny give, going to be awful?"

"Don't ask it that," Lucy says. "I don't want to know."

Too late. *Ask Again Later* stares back at me.

"Well, don't ask it again later," Lucy says. "Sometimes, I don't think that thing works anyway."

"So far, it's been pretty true," I say.

I shake the Magic 8 Ball again.

"Are they going to punish us today?"

Lucy covers her eyes with her hands, so I look.

Don't Count On It.

"See, Lucy?" I show her what it says.

Lucy looks somewhat relieved and then her face scrunches with worry.

"What?" I ask.

"Are they going to ground us, take something away from us or hurt us? If they don't punish us today, when will they? Are we going to get up every day wondering when, where and how it's going to happen?"

"I don't have an answer to that," I say. "I'd like to say they wouldn't do that, but knowing them, they probably would."

Sadness sweeps over us as we hug each other. Soon, we fall asleep. Sometime later, I awake with a start. It's dark out. I sneak out of bed without stirring Lucy, and turn on the light. Our chair is securely in place. That's a relief. No one has been in here while we were sleeping. I move the chair away from the door, and open it as quietly as I can. I look out into the darkened hallway. Nothing. No lights, no sound. I peek over the railing down into the living room. Same thing. Did they leave? What time is it? I reach for my bag and dig around inside for a watch.

"What time is it?" Lucy asks, rolling over to face me.

"Eight o'clock," I answer.

"Are they home?" she asks.

"I don't know," I answer. "Everything's dark."

"Are they in bed?" she asks.

"It's too early for them to be in bed," I say.

"You never know with them," she says.

"You have a point," I say with a half disgusted chuckle.

"I have to go to the bathroom," Lucy says.

"Me, too," I say. "Let's go together."

After we use the bathroom, we decide to sneak downstairs to investigate. Lucy hangs closely behind me as we descend the stairs. Thankfully, the street light on the corner shines inside the house enough so we can see without turning on the lights. I pull the living room curtain back and look outside. Danny's car is gone. What a relief. I feel Lucy's grip on the back of my shirt ease up.

"They're gone," I say.

"I'm glad," she says, "Are they out drinking? What's going to happen when they get back?"

"It means we put everything we can find in front of our door when we go back up," I say, half-heartedly, but kind of serious, too.

"I don't want to be here, Cart," Lucy says. "Can't we leave again?"

"We need to make a plan," I say. "We can't go back to the bus station. That old guy won't sell us tickets twice and Danny will find us again. I don't want to hitchhike. It's too dangerous."

"What are we going to do?" Lucy asks.

I can see the tears welling up in her sparkling, kaleidoscope eyes.

"We need to get our hands on some money," I say. "Freeport is smaller than Mason, but it's not *that* small. We can hide out for a while. We've been booted from the house enough times to know where everything is in this town. I bet Danny doesn't. I'm sure he only knows how to get to the bars and the liquor stores. We'll steer clear of them. Maybe we can get a motel. I saw one on the west end of town one day when we went to the park. Maybe I could pass for eighteen. That's all the older you have to be to get a room. I saw it on an advertisement. Once we hide out for a few days, I bet Danny stops looking. He doesn't care about us and will be glad to have us out of the picture. I'll call Ben. He drives a car. Maybe he'd come pick us up."

"Do you think he would?" Lucy asks, hope filling her voice. "That sounds like a perfect plan. But, how will we get money?"

"I'm still working on that," I say. "Maybe I could get a babysitting job in the neighborhood."

"That would be great," Lucy says. Her smile soon fades though. "What about me? I don't want to stay here without you while you babysit."

"I'll just tell whoever hires me that you are part of the deal too," I say. I hug Lucy. "We stick together, no matter what."

Lucy and I head to the kitchen to see what we can find to eat. We're sitting at the kitchen table snacking on crackers and milk when we hear the living room door open and smack shut.

17

"What the hell?" I mutter. I stand up and Lucy does too. She moves closer to me, whimpering.

"Shhh," I whisper. "Stay behind me and if we have to make a run for it, we'll go out the basement door."

In the dark, my ears tune in to every sound. I hear muffled crying into a pillow. Mama? I hear Danny's car revving down Float Street. We're going to get stuck here in the kitchen. I grab Lucy's hand and we sneak into dining room and head toward the stairs. Mama is crying on the couch and lifts her head when she hears us. She forgets about us when the door opens.

"What the hell, June?" Danny screams.

Lucy and I freeze in place at the foot of the stairs, still shielded by the dining room wall. Danny is on the other side of the wall. If we go up the stairs now, he'll see us. We barely breathe, waiting for their next move. Lucy's fingers are squeezing the blood out of my arm. I put my finger to my mouth to make sure she stays quiet. I hear Mama get up off the couch.

"Don't talk to me, Danny," Mama says. I hear her give him a push and he staggers backward. Great. He's fairly drunk if Mama can make him stumble.

"June, it's not what it looked like, I swear," he says. "That chick came onto me and I was telling her to hit the road, you know? I already got me a girl. You know I only dig you."

I roll my eyes. He is full of shit. Maybe, this is the chance we've been waiting for. She finally smartened up to Frank and Lumberjack Joe – well Joe smartened up to her. Maybe Mama will now see Danny for what he is – a lying, cheating, scum bag, and we'll go back to Mason and leave him here. The thought of this makes me feel brave. Maybe I can add to her doubts. I pop out from behind the wall. Danny jumps, not knowing we are there. Lucy is still clinging to the back of my shirt. I'm sure she's wondering what I'm doing.

"What the hell do you want?" Danny asks.

"Mama, Danny is such a pathetic liar," I say. "He hasn't been honest with you about me, or probably anyone else he's been around. I'm sure whatever you saw, looked exactly like what it was, Danny flirting and hanging on someone else."

"You shut up and get out of here," Danny says. "Or I'll take my belt off and whip the both of you."

I feel Lucy recoil and I have to admit, I take a step backward myself, until seeing the hesitation on Mama's face. Is she listening to me for once?

"Well, it's not the first time I've seen you do this," Mama says, turning to Danny. "Maybe, it's time the girls and I go back to Mason. This doesn't seem to be working."

"What do you mean?" Danny asks Mama. He looks over her shoulder and shoots me a cold, hard stare; like it's my fault he's getting busted.

"I have done nothing but take care of you and cook and clean for you," she says.

I cough out loud. That's even bigger bullcrap than what comes out of Danny's mouth. Mama shoots me the dirty look this time.

"You promised to take me ring shopping and you never did," she adds.

"June, Baby, you know I love you. Let's go upstairs and talk about it. These damn girls interrupted our day, if you remember. They stole my money and ran away. We had to find them, although I don't know why. We should have let them go wherever they were heading and be done with them."

"You were the one who was pissed and wanted the money back," Mama says. "I'm just tired of all of the drama with you and the girls. Clearly, you don't like them and they don't seem to like you. The girls and I should move and you can go back to the bar and that little tramp."

Wow. Would my Mama actually leave Danny for us? Has hell frozen over? I smile in Danny's direction. I feel like jumping up and down and doing a victory dance. Did we just win the lottery? And our prize is a bus ticket out of Danny's life forever?

Danny looks panicked for a moment, and then grins back at me. He feels around in his pocket, all the while staring me down. I swallow. What is he up to? Does he have a gun? A knife? Nothing could prepare me for what happens next. Danny pulls a ring out of his pocket. I am not an expert and I don't know rings, but this thing doesn't look new or even real. Almost like a cheap imitation. I wonder who it used to belong to and if he stole it. He makes sure I know what he has in his hand and what his intentions are. He stops staring at me and focuses on Mama. He gets down on one knee, and right then and there, asks my mama to marry him. Her face lights up.

"Yes," bounces off my ear drums.

She said yes? Danny stands up and Mama runs to him. He puts the ring on her finger. She looks down at it admiringly. Then, she goes in for the big, sloppy kiss and hug.

My mama just agreed to marry a man who is a liar, a cheater and a pervert. He has physically and sexually threatened me and now, he thinks we're going to call him Daddy? When hell freezes over and donkeys fly. I feel like I have been sucker punched in the gut, yet again. I lean back against the wall. I look down in defeat, and notice my mood ring is completely black. I'm sick and tired of seeing that color and am beginning to think it's broken. Only it's not broken, our life sucks.

Lucy sobs. The fear in her eyes breaks my heart. I can barely make sense of anything at this point. We are screwed. We need to make a plan and fast. Somehow, some way, we need to figure out how to get out of here, not get caught and never come back. I don't know how I'm going to make this happen. I'm sure defeat is plastered all over my face. Danny is winning. He must be thrilled. There's no telling what he will do now. As Mama hugs him, he looks over at me and Lucy and blows us an air kiss. I grab Lucy's hand and we turn and walk away. I hear Mama and Danny laughing.

"Hey, girls," Danny yells out. "Come back here. Where are our congratulatory hugs and well wishes?"

We don't say a word and we don't turn around. We go outside and sit on the front porch in the dark. The screen door slams like a prison door and we've just been handed our sentence. I pull the stupid mood ring off my finger and throw it as hard as I can into the middle of the street. It'll never be anything but black as long as we are living here.

18

Later that night, after Lucy falls asleep, I sneak out of our bedroom and close the door behind me. I sit down on the top step of the stairs, feeling numb. The house is dark. Mama and Danny are back at the bar drinking it up to celebrate their engagement. To think I almost had her convinced. I was so close. Why does she choose to believe Danny over me? Why would I lie about something like that? Will Danny go through with marrying Mama? And what if he doesn't and leaves? I guess it'll be the same as it has been with all of the other ones. They move on, and we're still here waiting for love and approval. Only nobody notices. Especially Mama. She's off looking for the next sorry guy. And what's *he* going to be like? He'll probably be another smelly, drunk pervert wanting to be with Mama at night while eyeing her daughters by day. Is sex with a guy that all-consuming and fantastic that you sell everyone and everything else out in order to get the attention?

What in the hell is wrong with Lucy and me that everyone wants to throw us away? Aren't we worth someone wanting to do the right thing for us?

I stand up and head down the dark hallway towards Mama and Danny's haven. I am determined to find money, or something, that will help us get out of here. I don't turn the lights on, in case they come down the street and I'm still in here. I know he keeps a penlight on his dresser. I pat my hand over the top of the dresser until I feel the light with my fingers. Picking it up, I turn it on and begin my search. There's got to be something that Lucy and I can use, or pawn, to get some money.

Maybe we'll try the bus stop again in a few days. I don't know. It might work this time. It's the fastest way to get out of here. We have to time it right. I'll get the bus schedule so I know to buy a ticket right before the bus is scheduled to come. We'll make sure we do it when Danny is at work. I'll tell that nosy, old man at the station, who thinks Danny is a good person, that my mama got sick and Danny drove to Mason to pick us up. I'll use my sweetest smile and most sugary voice. He'll fall for it. He thinks we're the perfect family. It's funny how easily some people can be deceived.

I begin my search going through Danny's dresser drawers. Believe me, rifling through his underwear again, is still disgusting, and ultimately, not worth the effort. I find nothing. I search through his T-shirts, and in the pockets of his jeans. Nothing.

I move over to Mama's dresser. I figure Mama doesn't have anything, but it doesn't hurt to check. I feel around her pajama drawer and find a stack of something hidden in the back. I pull it out of the drawer and shine the light on it. It's a stack of papers and photos wrapped together with twine. I'm a bit surprised. Mama isn't a sentimental person, and it's odd to me that she'd save anything.

I put the penlight in my mouth, so I can use both hands, and pull the twine off the stack and dig in. I find a pile of pamphlets on pregnancy, birth control, mental health, smoking and polio. Based on the way she behaves, it doesn't look as if she's read a single one of them. I wonder why she keeps them? Lucy and I should probably read up. It's the only way we learn how things are in the world. Mama doesn't take the time to inform us of anything. We learn it the hard way, either by her crappy parenting, her loser boyfriends or these pamphlets.

As I set them aside, I notice money sticking out of one of them. Leave it to Mama to hide cigarette money in a quit smoking pamphlet. I open it up and see it's a ten-dollar bill. I open each of the other pamphlets and find they all have ten dollars in them. There's a total of fifty dollars. Where did Mama get the money? She doesn't work. Would she have stolen it from Danny? That doesn't seem likely, as he probably would have accused us of stealing it. I'll bet it's grocery money. Danny is constantly saying he can't believe how few groceries we get for the money she spends. It sets him off on tangents of why do we girls have to live here because all of his hard earned money goes to feed us. I've overheard Mama tell him that Lucy and I eat all of the time, so he doesn't see all of the groceries that she buys. It makes me mad. We don't eat that much because there's never much to eat.

Obviously, she's been skimming cash from the grocery money. She must have bought a few things, pocketed the rest of the money and told Danny we ate everything else. And the Mom of the Year Award goes to our very own Mama. I decide not to take the money yet. I'll wait until I have a good plan in place. I don't know how often she checks her stash, and if I take it now, she'll figure out it's missing before I have a plan. I'll have to take my chances that it'll still be here once we're ready to leave. I look through the rest of the stack carefully in case there's more money. There's not. But I do find a picture of me and Lucy sitting on Daddy's lap. I must be about five and Lucy one.

I remember that red, polka dot dress. Daddy bought it for me. Right after that picture was taken, he took us out for ice cream. It was hot that day, and the ice cream melted and spilled on my pretty dress. I cried. Mama would have spanked me and yelled. I remember Daddy hugging me and saying, "*Cart Baby, it's only ice cream. It'll wash out, and if it doesn't, I'll buy you another dress.*" That was right before he went into the Vietnam War. I don't have good memories after that.

I shine the light on the picture and touch Daddy's face. A tear trails down my cheek. My heart aches to see him again. I notice behind the picture is a card. It's a Valentine's Day card to Mama from Daddy. The front has a picture of a boy sitting by a spaceship. It says, "Valentine, is there any space in your heart for me?" I open it up to find a poem Daddy wrote to Mama. I giggle as I read it. It's exactly what my daddy would say.

I'd buy you veggies
I'd buy you fruit
But we all know you dig my Brut

I can't stop smiling as I think about my daddy writing that card and how he says Brut is a chick magnet. I understand what that means now. I laugh. It's my daddy who's a chick magnet, not some stupid cologne. I keep the card and the picture of the three of us out of the stack and put the twine back around everything else, placing it in the drawer exactly how I found it. I put the card and picture in the pocket of my pajama bottoms and head for the closet. I pause and listen. No speeding, engine revving, or crazy perverts. Good. I have time to dig further.

I shine the penlight inside the closet. I stick the light in my mouth again, so I have free hands to do a quick search in the pockets of everything hanging on hangers. I find a couple of dollar bills and quarters. I add them to my pocket. I take the light out of my mouth and shine it toward the shallow end of the closet. There's a stack of car magazines four feet high and two stacks deep and wide. Danny couldn't possibly be dumb enough to put money in any of them. I decide if I come up dry searching everything else, I'll come back to these. I turn and shine the light in the far corner of the closet instead. It's pretty deep. Someone could almost hide a body back there. I shudder at the thought. My light casts creepy shadows in the closet corners and I hesitate to go any further, but my need for money, or anything that will help get us out of here, is stronger than my fear. I keep going, making my way past brown paper grocery bags filled with old papers, bills and clothes. I'm not sure whether I should take the time to go through all of those bags, so I pass by the bags in the front, deciding to push further towards the back. I see an old baseball bat and glove. It's hard to believe Danny ever did anything other than sit on a bar stool. Peeking inside another paper bag, I find a stack of nude girl magazines. Danny is such a pig.

As I shine the light farther back, my heart races when it catches on a metal box. It's partially sticking out from behind an old duffle bag. I make my way back there and sit down amid all of the junk, pulling the metal box out. It's about the size of a shoe box with a handle on top. There's a small metal tab that slides to open it. I slide it over, fully expecting it to be locked, but it's not. Why wouldn't Danny lock it? Maybe there's nothing of value in it, or maybe Danny never expected anyone to be digging in the back of his closet. I'm sure Mama doesn't come back here – she has her hands full skimming money off the top of the grocery allowance.

I open the lid, and catch my breath when I find a small, plastic zip bag full of diamond rings. The label reads cubic zirconia. Every single one of them look like the one Danny gave Mama. What in the hell kind of scam is he running? My guess is Mama is not the first one he's given a ring to, nor will she be the last. That might be good news for us. There's still hope yet that he'll buzz off. I eye the rings in the bag. I don't know what cubic zirconia is but it must be cheap stuff if Danny has a bag of them. I place the bag back in the metal box and return it exactly how I found it.

As I lift the duffle bag to put it back, I decide to take a peek inside. It's heavy. Curiosity gets the best of me. I unzip the bag and look inside. Books? My guess is Danny doesn't know how to read so why would he have books?

I take a book out. It has an old gray-brown cover. I can't make out the title or the author. I open it, attempting to leaf through the pages, but the pages are glued together. In the center of the book there's a cut out space, making a little cubby. Inside the cubby is cash; a big wad of rolled up cash. I find fives, tens, and twenties. This is some serious money. It's just what we need to get out of here. I have to give Danny credit for being clever. But he's not quite clever enough. Why would he put the book with the money in it on top of the pile and not at the bottom? I probably wouldn't have looked past the first book or two. You'll get what you deserve, Danny.

I start to feel a glimmer of hope. Then, I hear the front door open and slam shut. Crap. They're home. From the back of the closet, I couldn't hear the car pull up, but that slamming front door came through loud and clear. I put the money back in the book and place it back inside the duffle bag. Tossing the bag in front of the metal box, where I found it, I move quickly back through the closet. I turn off the penlight and place it back on Danny's dresser. Laughter echoes through the house. I hear them stumbling up the steps. They're getting close. Too close. I don't think I'm going to make it back to my room without them seeing me, but there's no way I'm going to wait it out in their closet. I decide to chance it.

I slide along the darkened hallway wall, hugging my back as closely to it as I can. Mama stumbles up the steps and giggles. Danny stops and braces her from falling. I use those extra seconds to my advantage and get to my door, softly opening it. I step inside and close it behind me. My heart is racing. The thought of Danny catching me is more than I care to think about. I don't know what he'd do to me. Lucy stirs behind me.

"Cart?" What's going on?" she whispers.

I turn toward her, and in the small amount of light streaming in from the window, hold a finger to my mouth. Mama and Danny are at the top of the steps now, right outside our door.

"I know I heard a door shut, June," Danny says.

If he opens our door right now, he'll send me flying across the room.

"I bet your little brats were snooping around, trying to steal my stuff again," he says. "I'm going in there."

I watch as the doorknob turns. I freeze in terror. There's no time to put a chair under the door. There's no time to come up with a plan. I brace myself for what's sure to be an ugly scene.

19

My heart is pumping so fast and loud, it's deafening.

"Don't you have better things to do right now?" Mama asks him.

He lets go of the doorknob. I hear them kissing and making weird noises. I take advantage of their distraction and race to my bed. I get in and pull the covers up over me and Lucy. We huddle close together, eyes shut. Danny opens the door and looks inside. I can feel him standing there, staring at us in the dark. Lucy and I don't budge even a fraction of an inch.

"You get yourself ready for me," he says to Mama. "I'll be there in a minute. I'm going to go to the bathroom."

What in the hell is he doing? Lucy and I are facing each other. We squint open our eyes, reading each others thoughts. Goosebumps pop up on my arms. It's hard resisting the urge to scream. Every noise is magnified ten times louder in my head.

Danny walks over to the head of our bed and bends down next to my ear. I can't breathe.

"I know you were just up."

His smelly beer and cigarette breath covers my face. I stifle a cough and lay completely still. I feel Lucy tremble and squeeze her under the covers.

"If I find anything missing in my bedroom, I will be back, and you and I will be going for a little ride."

I resist the urge to swallow. I know he'll hear it. He must already hear my heart pounding. It's deafening to me. He reaches out and runs his filthy hand down my hair and pauses. He wraps his fingers around a large chunk of it and pulls hard. I flinch. I can't help it. It hurt. He chuckles and moves his mouth closer to my ear, almost touching it.

"Just as I thought. You *are* awake and you *can* hear me," he whispers softly. His breath tickles my ear. I stifle an unwanted laugh.

"I think maybe the best way to deal with you, is through your little sister. I bet she'll be sweeter than you. She'll definitely be easier."

Lucy stiffens next to me. It takes every ounce of strength within me not to reach up and pull his greasy hair and wrap it around his smelly face, suffocating him. He lets go of my hair, stands and chuckles again as he walks toward the door.

"I'm going to check my shit," he says, opening the door. "If anything is missing or it looks like you've been digging around in it, I'll be back."

He slams the door shut behind him. He whistles his way down the hall.

The pressure of living here is too much. I can't stop sobbing. I can't take his threats any more, especially now that he's making them toward Lucy. I can't stand not knowing when he's going to strike or what's going to set him off. We need to get out of here.

Hopping out of bed, I turn on the light. I put the chair under the doorknob, hoping that if Danny does come back, he won't be able to get in. Heading back towards the bed, I pick up my bag and sit down. I reach in and take out my

Magic 8 Ball. Lucy is huddled in the corner watching me. I hate that she has to go through this. It's not fair.

Still sobbing, I shake it and ask, "Is Danny coming back in here tonight?"

Cannot Predict Now.

I hear Danny bumping around in his closet. My head throbs. Did I put everything back exactly how it was? Did I forget anything? I can't stand not knowing if he'll scream and charge back in here or if he'll sneak back like a predator coming in for the kill.

"Cart?" Lucy asks. "Why are you crying? You're scaring me. He says that stuff all of the time. We haven't done anything, right?"

"I was just in there, Lucy," I say, "while you were sleeping."

I take a deep breath. "I found this stuff."

I stand up and pull a couple of dollar bills and change from my pocket, as well as the Valentine's card and picture of Lucy, me and Daddy. Lucy takes the picture and stares at it.

"We look happy," she says.

"We *were* happy. And loved," I add. "We need to get out of here. It's going to get worse."

"Will Danny hurt me?" she asks.

"I don't know, but we're not going to stay and find out," I say.

Deep down, I know he will eventually hurt both of us. And I don't think it's going to be that long before it happens.

I don't hear Danny in the closet any more and I don't hear him in the hallway. He must have seen his stuff is still there, so went to bed. It's not going to be there for long.

"Tomorrow, when Danny goes to work and Mama is napping after her strenuous morning of beer drinking and magazine reading, we're taking it all and we're leaving," I say.

"Taking what all? Going where?" Lucy whispers a little too loud.

I shush her again and tell her it's important to be quiet. Danny could be standing outside our door listening in, waiting until we say something that tips him off, so he can barge in here.

"Mama's been skimming money off the top of the grocery allowance," I whisper. "She's such a liar. They deserve each other and can both rot in hell. She tells Danny we eat all of the food while he's at work, but I found a stash of money in her drawer that says otherwise. We're taking it."

Lucy is quiet. I think it must be sinking in just how crappy our Mama truly is. I hate that her childhood is ruined because of Mama and her loser boyfriends. At least I had Daddy and know what love is supposed to be like. I hope Lucy feels a little bit of that with me. I'd do anything for her. I'd take all of Danny's punishments, so she wouldn't have to take a single one. I'd die for her.

"How much does Mama have?" Lucy asks.

"She's skimmed fifty dollars so far. And I snooped in Danny's closet too," I say.

Lucy gasped. "Fifty dollars? No wonder we're always hungry. Were you scared going into Danny's closet?"

"I was scared as hell," I say. "But it was all worth it because I found a wad of money that'll take care of us for a long time. Hopefully, it'll give us time to find Daddy."

"Do you think we'll find him?" she asks.

"One way or the other," I say, "we're going to find out what happened to him. And if he's dead, we will figure out how to live on our own. We are *never* coming back here. Danny isn't going to get the chance to hurt us. Mama can pick up as many loser boyfriends as she wants. We aren't going to suffer through another one of them ever again. We have each other. No one is going to separate us or hurt us. Ever."

Lucy squeezes me. My eyes not only well up with tears of love but also a fierce protection for her. Tomorrow is the day we start our new life. Tomorrow is the day we change our path and turn in the crappy cards we've been dealt for some new ones. We are done being the throw away sisters.

Lucy lies back down and closes her eyes. She falls asleep with a smile on her face, something I haven't seen in a long time. I sit and watch her for a few minutes. I want more than anything in the world to be able to make this work, to do right by her. She deserves it. I deserve it. I reach into my bag for my Magic 8 Ball. I shake it and ask if we'll ever stop being the throw away sisters.

Signs Point To Yes.

I smile. Maybe, the tables will finally turn and things will go our way. Feeling confident, I shake it one more time and ask it if we're going to find our daddy.

Reply Hazy, Try Again.

Every damn time.

20

Lucy and I both wake up early. The sun is streaming in through the tiny window and lands warmly on our faces. Lucy smiles at me. I smile back but then remember what today is. I'm scared. Somehow, my confidence from last night has slipped away. I can't let that happen. I know we need to get out of here. I glance over at the door, making sure the chair is still holding it shut. It is.

"We're going to be ok," Lucy says, as if she has read my mind.

"You are so brave," I say, hugging her. "Sometimes, I wish I knew for sure."

"Cart," she says. "You are the bravest and smartest person I know. As long as we're together, we're going to be ok. Besides, anywhere has to be better than here."

She's right. No one can separate us and together we will not fail. So, we make our plan. We repack our backpacks with more clothes and underwear. We roll everything we can, instead of folding, because you can fit almost twice as much by rolling. It's a trick I remember Daddy showing me. We throw in a hair brush and take some soap and shampoo from the bathroom. We leave enough room at the top for food.

I'll keep the money, picture and card I lifted last night, in my macramé bag with the Magic 8 Ball. I don't feel great about stealing money, but I also don't feel great about how Danny has been treating us. If he'd been even a little bit nice to us, I would never have stolen from him.

And Mama, I have no words for her. She's no Mama and I can't help but think if she would have given us to Daddy when he was coming around to see us, maybe we all would have been saved. So, I don't feel as bad taking their money. I want to believe the money, along with the Magic 8 Ball, will bring us luck and help us succeed. I don't know what I'd do without the advice from my Magic 8 Ball. It's almost like having a parent who actually knows something.

Lucy still has peanut butter in her bag from the last time. Peanut butter stays good almost forever. We add a couple of sweaters and a pair of long pants just in case the summer nights get cool. I'm not sure where we'll be sleeping. I guess somewhere outside if we can't get a motel. I'm not sure how I feel about that. I'm not a big outdoor person but I'm grateful it's not winter. We'd be stuck here if it was. No one can survive outside for even a few short hours during an Illinois winter.

Once Danny leaves for work and Mama drinks herself into a nap, we'll grab the money, throw in some bread or whatever else we find and scoot out the basement door.

"How are we going to find Daddy?" Lucy asks.

"I've been thinking about that," I say. "At first, no one will know we took their money or ran away, so I figure we're probably safe until it gets dark. Until then, we could go to the courthouse and see if we can find any records of Daddy or maybe even his Mama."

"Would they have any records here of them?" she asks.

"I'm pretty sure Daddy said he was from Freeport and that his mama still lives here, but it's been so long ago I can't be sure. If they're not from here, maybe we can catch the bus to Mason before Danny gets off work and Mama wakes up. Then, we can check there."

"Do you think they'll show the records to us?" Lucy asks. "And do we have to find his Mama? I've heard the stories Cart, and they don't sound good."

"Daddy's mama can't be any worse than living here. She may be mean, but I doubt she would want to hurt us like Danny. I don't know if the courthouse will tell us anything." I pause and consider the options. "I guess all we can do is ask, and hope we find someone nice who's willing to help us."

"Ok," Lucy says. "And if we don't, we'll go to Mason. Maybe our friends there will be able to help us. But why do we have to do all of this while Danny is at work? If we run away, don't we have lots of time?"

"Once Danny gets off work and gets home, I'm sure he'll check his money. Especially since he thinks I was snooping in his stuff last night, which I was. Once he sees that it's gone, he'll be searching for us," I say. "He might go to the cops because we'll have stolen their money. We're going to have to be very careful. We can't get caught this time."

The thought of Danny hunting us down and finding us again scares the hell me. He won't be passive about our punishment this time. I fear for both of our lives, but I can't tell Lucy. I'll have to make sure she knows we both need to be very careful and aware. I wish I knew if Danny would go to the cops or not. It's one thing to be on the watch for Danny but adding the cops could really suck.

"Cart," Mama yells, from the bottom of the stairs. "Come here."

"Coming," I say. Lucy and I hide our backpacks in the closet and move the chair from the door. We both stand at the top of the steps, looking down at her.

"Danny is pulling a double shift today, so I want you to dust and vacuum our bedroom and clean the toilet and tub," she says. "And do a good job."

113

"I thought Danny didn't want us in his haven? Maybe you should do it. I don't want to get into trouble," I say.

"Like you're ever worried about getting into trouble," Mama replies. "Of course, Danny won't know you've been in there because he's going to think I cleaned it and you're not going to tell him anything different."

"Fine, Mama," I say.

And no, I'm not going to tell him anything different. By the grace of God, I'm never going to see him again. So, yeah, I'll clean his haven. It's perfect, really. Now I have an excuse to be in their bedroom!

"Let's clean the bathroom first," I say to Lucy. "That way, by the time we get to their bedroom, Mama will be out cold."

"You're so smart, Cart," Lucy says. "I hope I grow up to be as smart as you."

"I hope you grow up happy," I say. "You deserve to feel loved and to be happy."

"I do feel loved and I am happy when I'm with you," she says.

"If we find Daddy, it's going to be even better," I say. "I know it."

Lucy and I take our time cleaning the bathroom, giving Mama enough time to get drunk and pass out. I sneak downstairs to see what she's up to. Just as I thought, she's on the couch drinking beer and flipping through a magazine.

"Is the upstairs done?" she asks.

"We just finished the bathroom," I say. "We're cleaning the bedroom next."

"Good," Mama says. "And stay out of Danny's stuff while you're in there. He swears you were snooping in there last night."

"I was sleeping last night, Mama," I say. "I haven't been in your bedroom unless you've asked us to clean it."

I cross my fingers behind my back like that makes up for the little white lie.

"Go get me another beer," Mama says.

"Sure. Do you want two?" I ask, trying to rush the process.

"One is fine, Cart," Mama says. "I'm not a drunk."

Whatever, I think. I read the pamphlet. You were out half the night drinking and you're drinking again today. You'll most likely be drinking again tonight and tomorrow. No, Mama, that's not a sign of being an alcoholic, is it?

While I'm in the kitchen, I take the opportunity to scope out the fridge and cupboards. There's not much in either place, except for beer.

Grabbing the beer, I head back to the living room so Mama doesn't wonder what's taking so long. I can't risk getting her suspicious. Mama takes the beer from me, without saying thanks.

I debate on whether or not to clean the bedroom at all since we'll be leaving, but do it anyway. We need to buy more time before Mama's beer kicks in. We dust, vacuum and clean the nasty smoke off of the windows. I'm not touching their sheets. No, on second thought, I think I will. I strip the bed, fold the sheets into a wad and take them to the basement. I cram it all in the washing machine. I'm not sticking around long enough to put them in the dryer. Let them find their wet sheets sitting in the washing machine tonight when they're tired and wondering where we went with their money.

When I come back through the kitchen and dining room, I peek in at Mama. Sound asleep. The empty beers are by her side and the magazine is resting across her chest. It's her typical "Danny is at work" pose.

It's time. I climb the stairs to the haven for what is hopefully the last time ever and take Mama's money from her dresser. Shoving it in my pocket, I grab Danny's penlight from his dresser and make my way to the back of the darkened closet. Opening the duffel bag and book, I take the wad of money. Honestly, I'm kind of surprised it's still here.

115

I figured Danny would have hidden it somewhere else, just in case. He's full of hot air. He probably doesn't think there is any way I could have found this. Won't he be surprised? He is going to be beyond pissed, to the point of being extremely dangerous. It more than scares me. But staying here with him is even scarier.

I put the wad of money in my pocket, along with his penlight, and vow to be alert every moment of the day and night. We will not get caught and I *will* make a life for Lucy and me that we truly deserve. A devious smile curves my lips as I have a last minute thought. I'm sure my attitude and the things I say and do *are* what get me into more trouble, but I can't help it. I take the bag of high-class wedding rings from the metal box and shake them all over Mama and Danny's stripped bed. I almost wish I could stick around long enough to see how he explains his way out of that one.

21

Lucy and I are three blocks from the house before we feel like we can breathe. I wish I felt more relief at being gone. The fear of getting caught is overwhelming. I feel like a football is stuck in my throat. And the extra adrenaline is giving me a headache. We stop at the school playground. I'm glad it's empty. I hug my macramé bag a little closer to my side. It's where I put the money, Danny's penlight and my Magic 8 Ball.

"What are we going to do?" Lucy asks.

I take in a deep breath to help steady my nerves. There will be no saving either of us if we are found by Danny.

"I've been thinking about that," I say. "I might have a plan."

"You always do," she says, smiling.

"Yeah, well, sometimes they're not so hot," I say with a laugh, "but I think this is one of my better ones."

"Tell me!" she says.

"We're going to go to the bus station and sweet talk that old guy into believing whatever I come up with, so he'll sell us two tickets to Mason. Only, we won't be getting on the bus."

"Why not?" Lucy looks confused.

"Because Danny and Mama will go down there and that stupid, old man is going to tell them we got on the bus for Mason. Then, they'll drive to Mason looking for us, only they're not going to find us because we'll still be here!"

Lucy smiles. "You are so smart!"

"We have to be careful," I say. "We can't trust anyone. Maybe Danny will have the cops or his friends looking for us. We need to stay out of sight. At least if they think we're in Mason they won't be hunting for us here. Maybe we can get a motel room."

"Do you think we can?" Lucy asks. "How long will our money last if we spend it on motel rooms?"

"I haven't had a chance to count the money I took from Danny," I say. "We need to make it last. I don't know if a motel owner will get suspicious if two young girls come looking to rent a room or not."

"Would they rent us a room," Lucy asks, "and then call the cops thinking they have two runaways?"

"That's a good question," I say. "If they do that and send us back to Danny and Mama, well, I can't even think about that."

"Can't we tell the cops about Danny and how he's a sick pervert?" Lucy asks.

"I don't know if they'd believe us," I say. "You saw how convincing he was with the old guy."

I reach into my bag and pull out the Magic 8 Ball.

"Whatever you see, don't say it out loud," Lucy says, plugging her ears as she walks toward the slide.

As I shake it up, I ask it if Danny is going to catch us. *Signs Point To Yes.*

I shove it back in my bag and stand up to leave. Lucy joins me. She doesn't ask and I don't tell. We leave the playground and walk in silence as we head downtown to the bus station.

Soon, we're standing before the building with the same old greyhound dog leaping across the sign. I have the chills.

Who gets the chills in the middle of a hot summer day? I hope and pray we don't get caught again. Mama should still be sleeping and Danny should be at work until late tonight.

I look at Lucy, take a deep breath, put on my prettiest smile and open the big heavy door to freedom. We step inside and look around. There are a few people milling around. A kid is crying in the corner by his mama, who isn't paying much attention to him. That looks all too familiar. I turn my attention to the old man at the counter and smile even bigger as we approach him. He looks up from what he's doing.

"Well, hello there, Missy," he says, recognizing me immediately.

"Hello, Sir," I say.

"Whatcha doing back in Freeport?" he asks. "Didn't you just leave for Mason, wasn't it?"

"Yes, sir," I say, my fake smile is beginning to burn my cheeks. "Our Mama needed emergency surgery and our daddy came to Mason to pick us up and bring us back. He's so thoughtful that way."

"I could tell yours was a good family," he says. "So will you need two tickets back to Mason?"

"Yes, sir," I say. "Our daddy has to pull a double shift today. So, he can't drive us back."

"So how's your mama doing?"

"Sir?" I say. "Oh, right, um, she's doing much better, thank you. We thought she could recover faster if we stay with Grandma for a while. You know, let her rest in peace and quiet."

I try my best to cover from that slip. I almost forgot my lie. Lying sucks. It's hard to keep track of what you say, even when you've just said it. The old man pauses, and looks at me over the top of his glasses with what seems like a disapproving stare.

"It's been a scary week," I say. That much *is* the truth.

"I would imagine so," he says.

He fiddles with some paper work behind the counter. The 0606 bus comes in ten minutes. Good timing."

That worked out well. I didn't have time to get a bus schedule. I smile, as I pay once again for bus tickets that we won't be using. From this point forward, we're going to have to not be wasteful with our money. This is worth it though, to get Danny and Mama off of our trail. The old man hands us our tickets as another elderly man shuffles up to the counter. He walks through the door next to the counter and soon is standing next to our guy.

"Your shift is up, Bob," the new guy says.

"That it is, Fred," the old guy says.

"Well, girlies, you're all set," he says. "Hope this visit with your grandma is better than the last time around."

"Thank you, Sir," I say.

I'm almost afraid to turn around. It's all too fresh who was standing there the last time we did. Lucy and I turn together. We smile at each other. The coast is clear. No sign of Danny or Mama. Lucy has been glued behind me not saying a single word this whole time. I hear her release a long breath. I almost giggle. It's a nervous giggle more than anything.

"Hold up girls," the old man says, shuffling up next to us.

We both freeze in place, thinking our game is up.

"I don't like to see young'uns waiting around without an adult. There are too many weirdos out there. I'll wait with you until your bus gets here. That way I know you're safely inside."

Of all the luck! I hope he doesn't see the look of panic in my eyes. Lucy looks over at me, her eyes wide, questioning what we should do.

"Oh, sir, you don't have to trouble yourself," I say. "I'm sure you need to get home to your wife. Besides, it'll be here in ten minutes."

"Nonsense," he insists. "The Mrs. Will be fine. And I'd feel much better knowing you made it on the bus with no problems. I'll be but a minute. I forgot my lunch bucket."

He heads back to his desk area, and the other old man heaves his lunch bucket up onto the counter. While our guy is gone, Lucy and I have a quick conversation.

"What are we going to do?" Lucy asks.

The pressure of having to think fast is really starting to wear on me. It's either going to kill me or make me a genius.

"I guess we have to get on the damn bus," I say, while eyeing the old man.

"We can't go to Mason," Lucy says. "Danny will find us there."

"I know," I say. "We don't have a choice now."

"Ok, girlies," the old man says. "I see the bus coming down the street. Let's get you inside safe and sound and on your way to see your grandma."

"Thank you, Sir," I say.

I want to scream and tell that old man to leave us alone. He doesn't understand what we're up against. Instead I nudge Lucy and we both smile as we walk toward the door and open it to wait outside.

The bus pulls up and the loud brakes hiss to a stop in front of us. The smell of diesel makes Lucy and I both cough. It's a depressing smell to me. I can see through the windows, the bus is already fairly full of people. We're the only ones getting on here. The driver opens the door. I walk up the stairs first, Lucy follows close behind me. I reach in my bag for our tickets and hand them to the driver. I turn to see if the old man is still there. He is. He waves and tells us to have a good trip. The driver closes the door and tells us to take a seat. This is not going how I planned. Will anything *ever* go as I plan?

Lucy and I find an open seat a few rows back. The driver pulls away from the station as we sit down. Somehow, we

have to make this bus stop. I can't make myself look at
Lucy. I know she wants answers. I don't have any.

22

I sit in silence, thinking as hard as I can for a reason to make this bus stop. We can't leave Freeport. Mason is much bigger than Freeport and we could probably stay "lost" there for awhile, but I think Freeport is the key to finding my daddy. I'm not sure why. There's something in my memory about my daddy, Freeport and his mama.

I sneak a peek at Lucy. She is looking at me with her worried, 'what are we going to do face'. I sigh. Time. I need time to think. There is no time. The wheels on the bus keep rolling. We're now out of downtown. What the hell? Is that what it's like as an adult? You have to have a plan and think out everything while life keeps on rolling, not caring if you're ready for it or not? I'd rather be a carefree kid, who has fun and doesn't have to think too much about anything heavy or real. The last time I felt like that was when Daddy was around. Damn Mama and her boyfriends and damn Daddy for letting her win.

"Cart," Lucy whispers. "We need to do something."

"I know," I snap. I rub my throbbing temples with the knuckles of my fingers and close my eyes. I'm trying to picture something, anything in my mind that might work. I open my eyes as a vision plays out in my head.

"Ok," I say. "When I give the go ahead, I want you to start moaning and holding your stomach like you're going to throw up. Throw in a gag or two if you can."

Lucy hesitates.

"Either you have to do it," I say, "or, I have to. One of us has to get the driver to stop. Otherwise, we'll be going to Mason. I'm sure, come tomorrow morning, that old man will have spilled his guts to Danny. He'll be in hot pursuit of us before we can wipe the morning sleep from our eyes."

Lucy's eyes grow wide. I immediately regret saying that to her.

"I'm sorry," I say.

"I'll do it," she says.

Before I can say anything else, Lucy begins to moan softly, wrapping her arms around her belly. She rocks forward and backward, her moans growing louder and more painful sounding. She's gathering attention of those sitting around us. I'm impressed. I place my arm around her shoulders and ask her what's wrong.

"Cart, I need to get off of this bus," she screams. "I feel like I'm going to puke. It must have been what I ate for lunch."

She rocks faster and starts to make lurching, gagging noises.

"Sir?" I yell up to the bus driver.

He doesn't hear me. Lucy is going to town with the whole act now.

"Hey, driver," the man sitting in the seat beside us yells out.

The bus driver looks up into the mirror over his head and slows down.

"What's going on back there?" he asks. "We have a schedule to keep."

"This little girl here is sick," he says, pointing over to Lucy. "She needs to get off the bus."

124

"No can do. Once we get rolling, we don't stop until we get to Mason," he says.

Lucy hears this and turns it up a notch. Her gagging noises sound impressive even to me, and I know she's faking it. She begins rocking faster, with real tears streaming down her face, which is turning a weird shade of red.

Someone from the back yells out to get her off the bus before she throws up and contaminates everyone. The bus driver slows even more and pulls over to the parking lane on the street, bringing us to a stop. The air brakes hiss with dissatisfaction. The bus idles in park. The driver walks back toward us. I look at Lucy, encouraging her with my eyes to keep it up.

"Sir," I say. "My sister is not feeling well."

"I see that," he says.

"We only live two blocks from here," I say, as I comfort Lucy. "We are going to see our grandma in Mason, but I don't want to get grandma sick now. She's old. I need to take Lucy home to Mama. Please, let me take Lucy back home."

The bus driver stands there, staring at us, hesitating over what to do. As if on cue, Lucy doubles over and makes some more impressive gagging noises. Even I'm starting to feel a bit nauseous listening to her.

"For the love of God," someone else yells nearby, "let them off. I don't want the whole damn bus to smell like puke all the way to Mason."

"Where did you say you lived?" he asks.

I don't want to tell him our real address. I pause for a moment and look out the window. We're not far from the hospital, which is on Stephenson St.

"We live up on Stephenson," I say, "just a couple of blocks from here."

"All right," he says. "Grab your stuff. I never let people off my bus once they're on, but since your sister is sick, and we're just a couple of blocks from your home, I'll make an exception."

Lucy and I stand up and grab our belongings. I carry both of our bags as she wraps her arms around her stomach, doubling over a bit as we make our way down the aisle. Real tears stain her face. Someone claps as we leave. People are rude. What if Lucy had been sick for real and I needed help with her? Isn't there anyone in this whole damn world who cares about anybody but themselves?

The door closes shut behind us. The driver revs the diesel engine. The gears grind as he moves forward without us. The sound is deafening. A poof of stinky, diesel smoke shoots out and ruffles our hair as the driver powers up and heads down the road. The smell is not one I will ever associate with a good feeling. It will forever remind me of my fear and hatred of Danny and Mama. She should have protected us. She should have sided with us. She should have put us first. Now we are homeless, with stolen money and a Magic 8 Ball to see us through. I don't know how long we can live like this, or *if* we can live like this for even a day. But, my fear of getting caught by Danny is more powerful than what might face us on the streets of Freeport. At least, I think it is.

23

We don't waste time standing there on the busy street. The faster we move away, the better.

"Now what?" Lucy asks, as we head out.

I can tell by the tone of her voice that she doesn't want to ask. I think she can sense I don't know any more than she does at this point.

"First of all," I say, "that was some amazing acting back there on the bus."

Lucy stops walking and I turn to look back at her. She giggles and takes a bow.

"Thank you, thank you, very much," she says. "I wasn't sure I had it in me, but once I got started it seemed to flow naturally."

"I hope the schools in Freeport are big on drama classes," I say. "You clearly need to be on a stage."

Lucy and I continue down the street.

"It's getting late in the afternoon," I say. "Let's stop at the courthouse and see if we can find anything out about Daddy or his Mama, while Danny is still at work and it's safer to be seen."

Fifteen minutes later, Lucy and I are across the street from the courthouse, on the edge of downtown. We look around for signs of trouble, or anyone who looks like they might be looking for runaways. The coast looks clear so we cross the street.

Once inside the building, I ask an officer where we can find the records department. He turns and points straight ahead to the sign jutting out from a door. Good. It's right inside the courthouse doors. We don't have to wander all over the building. The less people who see us the better, not that Mama would think to come here. She doesn't want to find Daddy anyway, and she'd probably go to great lengths to avoid his mama.

Lucy sticks close by as I push open the doors to the records department. I hear a soft chime as we enter. Nobody looks over at us. A tall counter separates us from the handful of women working on the other side. There are several desks and cabinets for storage. A couple of the ladies are chatting about their kids or husbands and don't see us. It takes a few minutes of us standing there for anyone to notice. An older lady in a lime-green polyester suit sees us from her desk, stands up and walks over.

"May I help you?" she asks, attempting a slight, unconvincing smile.

"Um," I stammer. "I'd like to know if we can get some information."

"Information about what?" she asks, pulling a pencil from somewhere in her hair. She grabs a piece of paper and looks down at us from the top of her cat-eyed glasses.

"We're looking for information on our daddy and grandma," I say. "I believe my grandma lives in Freeport. I'm not sure if Daddy is alive or not. Would you have death records available?"

I feel Lucy tense up as I ask about death records. Maybe I shouldn't have asked about that, but I need to try and get all of the information I can.

"What do you mean you don't know if your daddy is alive or where your grandmother is?" the lady asks, judgment written all over her face.

My face reddens and Lucy recoils farther behind me.

"Our parents went their separate ways," I say. "We lost touch with Daddy after he went to Vietnam. I want to make sure he didn't die."

"What's his name," the lady asks, "and his last known address?"

"Jack Matthews," I answer. "I don't know his last known address. I guess with my mama and us in Mason."

"Mason?" the lady asks. "I won't have any records from Mason. We only have Freeport records here."

"I think our grandma lives in Freeport, so maybe he did or does too," I say.

The lady gives me a disgusted look but walks over to a file cabinet, opens it up and begins rifling through the files.

"I have no death record for a Jack Matthews," she says. "But that doesn't mean he didn't die somewhere else."

Isn't she a cheery, ray of sunshine? Is it written in a handbook somewhere that all adults must be rude and snotty to kids?

"Ok," I say. "Can you look up Eleanor Matthews?" I ask.

The lady rifles through the files again.

"No Eleanor Matthews in our death records," she says.

"Can you tell us where she might live?" I ask.

"Absolutely not," the lady says, pushing up her glasses and slamming the file cabinet shut. "We can't go about giving out private addresses willy nilly to anyone who walks in the door. Would you want people giving out your private information?"

"I suppose if the person looking was my daddy, I would," I snap.

"Well, I never…" the lady huffs away. "You'll get no more information out of me."

Lucy and I turn to walk away when a younger lady approaches the counter. She turns back to make sure the huffy lady isn't looking.

"There's a phone booth down by the plaza," she says. "Check in the phone book. If either of them have a phone in their house, they'll be listed in the book."

The lady smiles at us, with a genuine warm, friendly smile. I smile back.

"Thank you," I say. "We appreciate your help."

It's nice to know someone can be decent. Lucy and I leave the courthouse and make our way to the plaza. There, on the corner, is a phone booth. True to what the lady said, a phone book is hanging on a chain inside the glass booth.

Lucy and I both cram inside the booth. I haul the hefty book up on the ledge and open it up. Lucy flips open the coin return and looks for any dimes or quarters left behind. It's empty. I get to the M section and page through until I get to Matthews.

"Lucy," I say, excitement building in my voice. "There are two Jack Matthews in here! One lives on Oak Street and the other on Stephenson Street."

"Let me see," Lucy says, looking over my shoulder at the book. "Do you think either of them are him?"

"It's hard to say," I say. "It's a fairly common name. But, maybe!"

I scan up the page and look under Eleanor.

"There is an Eleanor listed on LaCresta Blvd.," I say. "I don't have a paper and pencil, do you?"

"No," Lucy says. "I forgot to pack that."

"That's ok," I say. "Can you keep watch for anybody walking by?"

Lucy watches for people coming near us, as I gently rip the Matthews page from the phone book. I fold it carefully, several times, stick it in my pocket and close the phone book.

"Is that legal?" Lucy asks.

"Probably not," I say. "But we're desperate. We've already stolen food and money. What's a page from a phone book?"

For the first time in a very long time, Lucy and I walk away with hope in our hearts and smiles on our faces.

24

Lucy and I sit on the plaza by the water fountain, admiring the cascading water. The coins glitter like diamonds in the bottom of the pool.

"I'm hungry," Lucy says.

"Me, too," I agree.

The smell of grilled burgers from the Sizzle Shop restaurant across the plaza fills the air. We decide since we've had good luck with the phone book, we'll treat ourselves to a burger. Walking over to the restaurant, we head inside. It feels good to get out of the heat.

We take the first booth by the door in case we have to make a quick exit. We throw our backpacks into the booth and then, each take a side and slide in. I hold onto to my macramé bag. It has our money and my Magic 8 Ball in it. I sit facing the door, so I can see who comes in or walks by.

I look around the restaurant to see who's here. There's a mom and her little boy sitting a few booths back. There's also a grubby-looking, homeless guy, with an equally filthy backpack slung across one of his shoulders. It must hold his whole life in it. I guess he and I have something in common. I hold onto the strap of my macramé bag a little tighter. The homeless guy is drinking a coffee at the counter, not far behind us. He reminds me of someone but I'm not sure who. I wonder if he's one of Mama's long-lost boyfriends. He turns to look at us and stares. I look the other way. His long, dirty-blonde hair is clumpy and gnarled. His skin, sunburned and dry. He's clearly been at this homeless thing a lot longer than we have. It scares me. Will Lucy and I end up like that? There is something unsettling about him.

"Hi," a young waitress says, approaching our booth. She's carrying two glasses of water and two menus, which she places in front of us.

"Hi," I say back. Lucy smiles slightly, but doesn't say anything. I hate that everything she's been through has caused her to be so distrustful of other people. I hope one day that changes.

"Do you need a minute to look at the menu?" the waitress asks.

"No. We'll each have a cheeseburger with ketchup and pickles and share an order of fries. And we'll have the water to drink."

She writes our order down, grabs the menus and walks away.

"Where are we going to stay tonight?" Lucy asks.

"I'm not sure yet," I say. "I don't know if we should spend the money to stay at a motel or not. Maybe we should check out those addresses when we leave here."

"I don't know if I want to stay outside," Lucy says, "in the dark."

"We're probably safer at night then we are during the daytime," I say, "at least from Danny and Mama."

"What about raccoons and other night animals?" Lucy asks.

"They're more afraid of us then we are of them," I answer.

"Everybody says that," Lucy says, rolling her eyes. "I don't think it's true. I think it's something people say when they don't have answers. Or don't want to have to tell you, yeah, you're right. They're probably going to attack you and eat your eyeballs."

Lucy bugs out her eyes. I laugh. She brings me so much happiness. I hope I do the same for her. I want us both to be able to laugh at the things everybody else laughs at. Usually, there's not much in our life that's funny.

"Here you go," the waitress says, placing a plate in front of both Lucy and I.

We smile and sniff the delicious smell of grilled burgers. Danny's hockey pucks have nothing on these burgers. The waitress places the fries between our two plates along with a red squeeze bottle of ketchup.

It doesn't take long for us to devour it all. We both sit back in the booth, satisfied, full and feeling pretty content. The waitress comes back and asks if we want anything else. When we tell her no, she totals our bill and leaves it with us.

I reach into my macramé bag and pull out a ten-dollar bill. I take it to the register to pay. I leave the bag and rest of the money with Lucy at the booth. When I return, not two minutes later, my bag is gone.

"Lucy," I ask. "Did you move my bag over by you?"

Her eyes grow wide. "No," she says. "Didn't you take it with you?"

My heart sinks. "No. I left it on the seat right here."

I point to the empty space, then turn and look around the restaurant. The lady and her little boy are still in the booth eating their meal. I glance at the counter behind us and see that the homeless man is gone.

"Lucy, did the man who was sitting at the counter come over here by our stuff?"

"I didn't see him," she says. "But I dropped my napkin on the floor under the booth and slid down to get it."

"Stay here," I say to her.

I run out the front door and look up and down the plaza. I don't see him anywhere. I fight back the rush of tears burning at the corners of my eyes. He's gone and so is our money along with our only chance of making it. I walk back inside the restaurant. The waitress is standing by Lucy.

"I think that homeless man stole my macramé bag," I say.

"I'm sorry, Cart," Lucy says. "Don't be mad at me."

"Lucy," I say. "It's not your fault."

Lucy is crying, realizing the seriousness of our money being gone. I think about my Magic 8 Ball, the one thing that I could count on to guide me through this crap of a life. Right, wrong, or otherwise, it gave me comfort. I slump down in the booth. No money and no Magic 8 Ball. No picture of Daddy. No funny Valentine's card. Whatever happens, we will not go back to Danny and Mama. That much I DO know without the help of the 8 Ball. We can't go back to them. Not if we want to survive. But is the homeless world going to be any kinder? Not so far, by the looks of it.

"Can't anything ever go right?" I say. I feel completely defeated.

"Did you see him take the bag?" the waitress says.

"No," I say.

Lucy lowers her head.

"He comes in now and then when he can scratch together enough money for coffee," the waitress says. "I can call the police if you want. You can file a report. Maybe they'll catch him and you'll get your stuff back."

"Yeah, Cart," Lucy says. "That's a good idea. We can get our stuff back."

I look over at Lucy, wondering if she forgot we are on the run and that we stole money from Danny. Involving the police is probably not in our best interest and will only get us into more trouble.

"No," I say. "That's ok. There really wasn't anything of much value in the bag."

Lucy looks over at me confused.

"We better get going," I say. "Thanks for lunch."

The waitress tells us if we change our minds, she'll talk to the police with us. Fat chance that's going to happen. Once

Danny gets off work and realizes his money and Lucy and I are gone, he'll be at the police station. He will be pissed. I think I'd rather face the police than him. The homeless guy will end up off the hook and Lucy and I will be the ones getting arrested. I'm sure Danny will tell the police that he and Mama can "straighten us up".

We pick up our backpacks and leave the Sizzle Shop. I feel naked without my macramé bag. As the heat smacks us in the face, so does the reality that we are screwed. Lucy and I wander down the plaza. Our eyes are peeled for the homeless man. If I ever see him again, he's going to wish he stole anyone else's bag but mine. Once again, Lucy and I need to scramble to make another plan.

25

After Lucy and I leave the downtown area, we take the side streets to where I think the first Jack Matthews' house might be. Freeport is not ginormous, but there are a lot of little side streets. Hopefully, we'll find the right house and the right Jack Matthews. Could we be that lucky? Probably not, but I hope this time will be the exception.

I dream we find our daddy; he's off drugs and alcohol, is healthy, and extremely happy we found him. He'll hug and kiss us, saying he's been trying to find us all along. He'll say he can't believe how grown up, smart and pretty we are. I bet he'll tease us and tell us we better not have boyfriends because now they'll be answering to him. We'll play our favorite Beatles music and watch the bobbleheads and dance and laugh. We'll live like a family is supposed to live, with love and respect. We'll tell him about Mama and her string of boyfriends, especially Danny, and how he treats us. Daddy will be so angry, he'll hunt Danny down, beat him up and call him a dip stick and a candyass, just like I knew he would.

"Cart," Lucy says. "You've been so quiet. Are you mad at me?"

I shake the happy thoughts of Daddy out of my head and look at Lucy. She looks so sad. I know she feels responsible for our money being stolen.

"No, I was just thinking about how wonderful it would be to find Daddy," I say, stopping to face her. "I could never be mad at you. It's not your fault the money is gone. Please don't feel like it is. It won't solve our problems or make things better. That homeless man was hell bent on taking our stuff and he would have done so, no matter what."

"But I should have been watching it better," Lucy says.

"I'm the one who left it on the seat," I say. "It's my fault."

"But you left it for me to watch, and I didn't," Lucy counters.

"See how this is getting us nowhere?" I say. "Yes, it sucks that our money is gone, but we have our clothes and the food we put in our backpacks. We'll be fine. I have a little over five dollars from the change from our dinner, so that might come in handy for something. Maybe we'll find help before we run out of everything."

"Are we almost there?" Lucy asks. "My feet are getting tired and it's so hot."

"I know," I say. "I was sure Oak Street was around here somewhere."

We have been wandering around the streets of Freeport for over an hour. I guess I should have ripped the map out of the back of the phone book, too. We can't go back now. There are too many people downtown. We can't take the chance of being seen down there again. I don't know how late Danny is working. If he's already off work, he's looking for us. The cops might be too.

I don't know if it's a curse or a blessing that it stays lighter longer in the summer. Part of me wants it dark so we can sneak around without as much worry. But the dark brings its own set of problems – creepy people and scary night animals. It must be close to seven. The sun is not as hot and is setting. Mama must be awake by now. It's past dinner time. She's probably hungry and wondering what Lucy and I are going to fix for dinner. I wonder if she'll miss us or only what we did for her.

Won't Danny be disappointed when he gets home tonight and finds no dinner waiting for him? He better get used to it, because that's what he's going to get every night from now on. Nothing. And it's just what he deserves. And Mama, she deserves the same. Nothing. Danny's going to figure out in a hurry that it wasn't Mama who cooked, cleaned and did the laundry.

"Cart," Lucy says. "There's Oak Street over there."

She points across the street at the sign.

"Good eye, Lucy," I say. "Now we just need to find 1121."

We walk further down the tree-lined street and then we see it. 1121 Oak. I stop in my tracks.

"I don't think anyone lives here," Lucy says. "Or if they do, it's pretty sad."

"Well, that would fit the daddy I knew back then," I say, "but you're right, I don't see how anyone is living here."

Lucy and I cross the street and walk up to the house. Faded, metal letters hanging crooked on the porch post, tell us it's 1121. The screen door is dangling half off its hinges and the paint on the wood frame of the house is so peeled and faded, it's hard to tell what the original color was. Plywood covers the windows in the front of the house. The porch has missing planks. We can't get to the front door, much less inside. But, I want to get inside. I need to see if I can find signs of something that says my daddy might have lived here, or God forbid, still does.

We walk around to the side of the house, hoping to find a window that has glass in it so we can peek inside. There's a side porch with a door. I look around for neighbors who might be watching. There aren't any, and the tall fence beside us is flanked with overgrown shrubbery, blocking anyone's view of us. I head for the stairs.

"You're not going in there, are you?" Lucy asks.

"If I can get inside, I am," I say.

"It's going to get dark soon," she says.

"I won't be long," I say. "I just want to look around on the main floor. I have Danny's penlight."

I reach into my backpack and dig around.

"Crap," I say. "The penlight was in my macramé bag."

"See?" Lucy says. "That means you shouldn't go in. You won't be able to see."

"I won't go too far inside," I say.

I walk up the steps. I cup my hands around the glass on the door, peeking inside. It looks like the kitchen. I see cupboards, with most of the doors missing. Garbage and food containers are scattered all over the place. I twist the doorknob and push on the door. It doesn't budge. I kick it with my foot. Nothing.

"Let's go, Cart," Lucy says. "This place gives me the creeps."

"I can't get in anyway," I say. "It looks like a bunch of garbage. If Daddy did live here, all that is left behind is junk."

"Where's the other house at?" Lucy asks.

I come down from the porch and we make our way out to the front of the house. I pull the page of the phone book from my pocket and unfold it.

"Ok, the next Jack Matthews lives at 2360 Stephenson Street," I say. "It's probably going to take twenty minutes to walk there. Will you be ok?"

"I'm thirsty," she replies.

"Me too," I say.

I look around and notice a hose at the house next door. It's hooked up to the spigot.

"We can get a drink there," I say, pointing to the house next door.

"What if they catch us?" Lucy asks.

"Maybe they're not home," I say. "We'll just have it on long enough to get a drink and then shut it off."

We sneak over to the hose, turn it on and drink until we're full. It started out kind of warm, but then turned cold and tasty. We turn the water back off and make our way to Stephenson Street. It doesn't take long for us to get to the hospital at 2000 Stephenson. I'm feeling nervous. I SO want this to be Daddy. I wonder what my Magic 8 Ball would say. Even though every time I ask it if I'm going to find my daddy, it says *Reply Hazy, Try Again.* I'm almost grateful I don't have to see that answer now. All the same, I miss having it.

26

Lucy points to a small, white, boxy house in front of us. It's nothing fancy, but it doesn't look abandoned either. My heart starts to race. We stand there eyeing it for a few minutes.

"It says 2360. Are we going up?" Lucy asks. "Or are we going to stand here and stare at it?"

"Geez, Lucy," I say. "Impatient much?"

"I'm tired of walking, Cart," she says. "Let's do this."

I know Lucy doesn't remember Daddy nor have the emotional attachment I have, so this isn't as difficult for her. But she's right. We need to do this. I grab her hand, more for support than anything. She squeezes mine back and gives me one of her sweet smiles. Her kaleidoscope eyes sparkle like her smile. She gives me strength. We can do this. We walk up to the front door and ring the bell. I can hear movement inside.

"Someone is in there," Lucy says.

"I hear them too," I say.

The footsteps get louder as they approach the door. My pounding heart feels like it's going to burst out of my chest and splatter on whoever answers the door. That probably wouldn't make a good first impression. I want to vomit, cry and laugh at the same time. When the door opens, my heart sinks. Lucy moves behind me.

"I'm sorry," I sputter. "We are looking for Jack Matthews."

"I'm Jack Matthews," he says. "Do I know you?"

"But you're an old, black man," Lucy blurts, peeking out from behind me.

"Yes," he says, with a hearty chuckle. "Been black all my life and just recently getting old."

His eyes sparkle and he smiles a toothy grin. I try to smile back, but instead I cry. I stand there on his doorstep and have a complete mental breakdown. I am sobbing uncontrollably like a five-year-old child. All of these years of wondering, waiting and worrying, putting up with Mama and her crappy boyfriends, and we're still no closer to finding Daddy.

Now, we are homeless, with Danny probably stalking us and we have no money. There are no more options. I am out of ideas. Hope is what drives people forward. But tonight, on this man's doorstep, I lose my hope.

My tears turn into the ugly, snot-cry level of my downward spiral. I'm a mess. Lucy moves from behind me to my side, eyes wide, sad and confused.

"Cart," she says, putting her hand on my hand, "we'll find him."

She laces her fingers in mine. A tear slides down her face.

"Martha," Jack yells into the house, "we have a situation. Can you come here?"

Through my tears, I see a large, black woman come to the door. I see kindness and concern on her face as she eyes Lucy and me up and down.

"Don't just stand there, Jack," she says. "Bring these poor babies into the house and get them a glass of lemonade."

Jack moves to the side, motioning for us to enter. Normally, I wouldn't go into a stranger's home, but I'm completely wiped out and it's hot. A glass of lemonade sounds good. I know crappy people when I seen them, and I don't get that vibe from Jack and Martha. Lucy and I walk inside their home. Martha pulls a handkerchief out of her sleeve and offers it to me. I half-heartedly smile and take it from her. I wipe my eyes and blow my nose as she guides us to her kitchen table. She pulls out a seat for both Lucy and I and we sit down. Jack brings over two tall glasses of lemonade and a plate of sugar cookies.

"Now," Martha says. "You tell me what this is all about."

I take a drink of lemonade, breathe deeply and unload our entire life story on Jack and Martha, right there at their kitchen table. I don't know why I did. I don't know them. This stuff has been pent up in me for so long, I have to get it out. If feels good to tell somebody. They don't interrupt, but listen with genuine concern until I finish. Martha's handkerchief is loaded up with tears and snot, but I am feeling better than I have since I can remember.

I pause, take a long drink of lemonade and wait and see what happens next. Lucy has tears streaming down her face. Some of what I've said she's never heard before, but most of it she knows. I feel bad, but once I started talking, it just fell out of me.

"I'm sorry, Lucy," I say. I get up and walk over to her and hug her. "I know some of this is probably shocking to you."

"I know most of it," Lucy says. "Sometimes, when you thought I wasn't paying attention, I was. And when you thought I wouldn't understand, I did."

"I was afraid of that," I say. "You are so brave and smart."

"If it wasn't for you," Lucy says, "we would be far worse off than we are. Danny would have succeeded and Mama would have been in denial. It never would have ended. We had to get out of there."

We hug again and then turn to look at Jack and Martha. They're standing there staring at us, trying to process everything I unloaded.

"Oh, Jack, honey," Martha says. "You better get us a glass of lemonade, and put a little pick-me-up in ours. Make a couple of PB&J sandwiches for these two, while you're at it."

Jack does as Martha says. She motions for us to sit back down and pulls out a chair to join us.

"Do you think we should call the police?" Martha asks.

"No!" I yell, startling her. "We stole Danny's money and then someone stole it from us. We'll be in trouble for stealing it. They won't care or listen to the reasons why."

"I think under the circumstances, if you tell the police what you've been dealing with, they'd overlook certain things. You *are* minors. We have a friend on the police force we could call."

"No!" I yell again. "If you're going to do that, we have to leave right now."

I stand up and look at Lucy, who reluctantly stands up too.

"Now, now, child," Martha says. "You two sit back down and relax."

"We can't prove anything," I say, sitting back down. "It's his word against ours. And believe me, that greasy snake in the grass can be very convincing when he wants to be. We saw it in action at the bus station the first time we tried to get away."

"So, what's your plan?" Martha asks.

"I'm not sure yet," I say. "We might have some time before they realize we're still in Freeport. They're going to think we got on the bus and went to Mason. That is, if they bother to check the bus station and ask questions. They probably will though, since we took their money. I wonder if we wouldn't have taken their money, if they'd even care we were gone?"

Jack rejoins us and sits down. He places a sandwich in front of Lucy and me. We don't waste time eating it. He slides Martha a glass of lemonade and takes a swig of his own.

"I think you need to get the police involved," Jack says. "You can't roam the streets of Freeport."

"That is true, you can't," Martha adds. "Tonight you both can stay here and in the morning, we'll help you figure out a plan."

I look over at Lucy to see her reaction. She's smiling.

"Ok," I say. "We'll stay here tonight. Thank you. And no police, at least not right now. Can we stay together in the same room?"

"Sure can, Sweetie," Martha says. "Our spare room has a big bed you both can share if you'd like."

"We had to share a twin bed at home," Lucy says, her sparkly eyes twinkling. "Cart takes up a lot of room and makes me sweaty when we sleep."

I laugh and so do Martha and Jack.

"I think it was you who were making me sweat," I say, teasing back.

"I think everyone has had a very long day," Martha says. "It's time for you children to get some sleep while Jack and I help you figure out what to do."

"Ok," both Lucy and I say.

It's nice having someone take over and be the parent. I feel safe here. It's a feeling I haven't felt since Daddy was around.

27

Martha walks Lucy and me down the hallway and shows us to our room for the night. She reaches inside for the switch on the wall and flips it on. I stare in awe at the bright bedspread on the bed. It spans a vibrant array of colors and hangs down the sides like a beautiful rainbow.

"You two make yourselves at home," Martha says. "The bathroom is straight across from your bedroom if you need it. She turns and points out the door. "Sweet dreams. See you in the morning."

She gives each of us a bear hug with a sweet smile.

"And don't you worry about nothing tonight. Just sleep and know that you are safe."

Martha turns and shuts the door on her way out. I look at Lucy, who is kicking her shoes off and climbing on the bed without a care in the world. I notice behind the bed there's an oversized painting of a black Jesus on the wall. I've never seen a black Jesus before. I stare at his face. I don't know why he's always shown as white. It doesn't seem fair if you ask me. The black Jesus looks just as nice as the white Jesus. The wall opposite of the door is loaded with family pictures. They must be of their children, grandchildren, cousins, aunts and uncles. They cover the wall almost completely. And everyone is smiling large, toothy smiles. Real smiles. You can tell they're real because they reach all the way up to their eyes. It makes them sparkle in a way nothing else can. I find myself smiling too, looking at all of those happy faces, holding hands and hugging. How nice it must be to belong to a family like this one. I think of the picture of Lucy, Daddy and me, that was stolen. Our eyes sparkled then. Will we find that kind of happiness ever again?

The colors in the painting on the opposite wall draw my attention. I can't stop staring at it. Four black ladies in long, colorful dresses with matching poufy hats, face outward while dancing in a circle, their hands held up to the heavens. The dresses are the most beautiful colors of orange, pink, yellow and blue that I've ever seen. We've never had anything like this on our walls at home. I feel like there's a whole history or culture here that I'm missing out on.

"We should get our pajamas on," I say to Lucy.

I turn on the lamp on the nightstand, and walk over to the wall, flipping off the overhead light. Lucy reluctantly gets out of bed and we rummage through our bags for a pair of pajamas. Putting them on, we get settled in bed under the covers. I reach over to the nightstand and turn the light off. A small patch of light from the moon peeks through the curtain opening.

"I can hear them talking in the kitchen," Lucy says.

"I know," I say. "I hope they stay true to their word and not involve the police."

"They wouldn't do that, would they Cart?" Lucy asks.

"I hope not," I say. "I don't think I could handle the betrayal of one more person."

Lucy and I listen to Jack and Martha talk a little longer. Their voices fade, and then we hear the soft music of Nat King Cole singing, *Unforgettable*. I sneak out of bed. Opening the door, I peek out. Jack and Martha are dancing sweetly in each other's arms. They must still be in love after all of these years. I can't imagine what that's like. I close the door and make my way back to the bed. Climbing inside, I snuggle under the covers with Lucy, falling asleep feeling safe, peaceful and surrounded by love. It's funny how that can happen in an instant around some people, and never in a lifetime around others.

~

I awake in the morning with the sun streaming in through the window. I peek over at Lucy, who is still sleeping. She looks peaceful. It's a relief not to see worry plastered across her sweet face. She is far too young to know worry as well as she does. I hope some day Danny's perverted behavior catches up with him and he goes to prison. I hope the men in prison are worse to him than he was to us. My Daddy says we should never wish bad on anybody for any reason, but I have to wonder if he wouldn't be ok with this. It would serve Danny right.

Lucy stirs as I stretch my legs under the covers. I try to block the thoughts floating into my head about what we're going to do next. I want to enjoy this feeling of being cared for as long as we can. I wish we could stay here with Jack and Martha but I'm not sure if that's possible. We're minors and we ran away from home, not to mention stole money. The odds of anyone letting them keep us are probably not in our favor. I'm sure if Danny and Mama find out we're here, they'd come for us and punish us. I'm sure they'd make up some convincing lie and everyone would think they're the best parents in the world. Except for Jack and Martha. They'd still believe us, wouldn't they?

I snuggle next to Lucy, enjoying the comfort of the bed and the beauty of the pictures on the walls, a little while longer. I wonder if we'll be sleeping outside tonight. I don't know how Lucy is going to handle that. I have to admit, the thought of sleeping outside without any kind of protection scares me, too.

149

"I smell bacon," Lucy says, rolling over, smiling in my face. "I can't remember the last time we got to eat bacon."

"I guess I was so wrapped up in my thoughts, I didn't notice," I say.

"Who doesn't notice bacon?" Lucy asks. "Weirdo."

I laugh at her. Weirdo is pretty close to the truth.

"I guess we better get dressed and check it out!" I say.

Lucy and I waste no time leaping out of bed. We take our pajamas off, roll them up, put them in our backpacks and get dressed. We pull the covers up on the bed, and make everything neat and orderly so Jack and Martha think we're helpful and well mannered. Maybe that will sway their decision in wanting to keep us a while longer.

"Good morning, girls," Martha says with a hearty smile, as we head toward the kitchen.

"I figured the smell of bacon would bring you out sooner than later. You *do* like bacon and eggs, peanut butter toast and chocolate milk, right?"

"Boy, do we ever," Lucy says. Her eyes have never looked so sparkly and full of life and energy.

"Sit down, sit down," Martha motions us to the chairs. "You can start on the peanut butter toast and chocolate milk. I'll bring over the bacon and scrambled eggs in a minute."

We don't waste any time sitting down and digging in. I don't know why it is, but food always tastes better when somebody else fixes it. Unless, of course, it's Mama cooking. Cardboard is tastier than her cooking.

"Where's Jack?" I ask in between bites of toast. I wash it down with a big swig of chocolate milk and smile. I could get used to this.

"Oh, child, that Jack is an early morning riser," she says with a chuckle. "He's up and at 'em before old Mr. Sun even knows he's on deck to make an appearance."

Lucy and I laugh. That will never be either one of us. Martha brings over a heaping plate of bacon and enough scrambled eggs to feed half of Freeport. She instructs us to eat until we're full, and we obey. Lucy and I are both in a semi-food coma when Jack enters.

"Good morning one and all," he says with a cheerful smile. "It smells good in here. Hope you all saved me some."

"It's a good thing you came when you did," Martha says with a wink. "I thought these girls were going to eat the plates."

She chuckles a hearty laugh and for some reason I panic. My face crumples into a frown. Maybe we ate more than we should have. That's not going to make them want to keep us.

"Did we eat too much?" I ask. "I'm sorry. We won't eat anything else today. I still have a few dollars the homeless man didn't steal; I can pay you for the food. Do you want us to leave now? I understand if you do. I'm really sorry."

Lucy looks at me as tears well up in her eyes. Her sparkle is gone. She pushes her plate away and looks remorseful.

"Oh, Sweet Jesus," Martha says. She rushes over to us, hugging and squeezing, half in tears. "I am teasing you. I am so sorry. I forgot that you've gone through things you sweet babies never should have had to go through. Please forgive me."

Now, it's Martha's turn to tear up. Jack is speechless and I feel like an idiot.

28

Lucy regains her sparkle and sense of humor first. "Glad that's settled," she says, looking around at each of us. "I want more bacon."

She slides the plate back towards her and digs into the pile of bacon. I giggle. Martha turns her head and chuckles, her ample bosom heaving up and down.

"Never a dull moment around here," Jack says, lifting a piece of bacon off of Lucy's plate.

"You're brave," Martha says to Jack. "I'd watch out for that one. She's liable to think your fingers are juicy pieces of bacon and make short order of them."

Martha chuckles in the deep, friendly way she has about her, but stops short when she looks out the window. I see her look over at Jack and nod toward the window. The crease between her eyes deepens. I look out the window to see what's causing it. A cop. A cop has pulled up in front of the house. He gets out of his squad car and makes his way up the sidewalk.

"What the hell?" I say. "You called the cops? I thought we could trust you. Lucy, we have to get out of here."

I stand up and grab a hold of Lucy's hand, pulling her away from the table. She grabs a piece of bacon with her free hand and shoves it into her mouth. I'm gauging if we can run to our room fast enough to get our stuff and get out of the door before we are caught.

"Now, hold up," Jack says. "That's my friend, Frederick."

"Did you tell him about us?" I ask.

Jack looks down and sighs. "I did mention the situation this morning at coffee. I trust Frederick. I needed to find out if there was something Martha and I could do to help you. Maybe even keep you until this gets settled."

"What did you tell him about us?" I ask.

"I didn't go into all of the details," Jack says. "All I told him is that I am aware of a couple of girls who are running away from a pretty crappy situation at home and wondered what I could do to help."

"And?" I ask. "What did he say?"

"He said if they're minors they should probably be turned over to DCFS," Jack says. "Until, that is, they can figure out exactly what is going on."

"DCFS?" I scream. "Is he coming to take us to DCFS?"

"What's DCFS?" Lucy cries, our faces both struck in fear.

"No," Jack says. "He's here as a friend to talk to all of us."

The doorbell rings. I don't have a good feeling about this. Normally, I trust and like the police. They're on our side. But this time, it's different. I stole money. I'm a criminal. I don't care if I get punished for it, but I don't want Lucy to get punished. And if I have to go to jail, where will Lucy go? She can't go back to Mama and Danny. Oh, my God, I can't even think that. Without me there, Lucy will most definitely become a victim of Danny. We can't get separated. We will not survive if we get separated.

"Hi, Frederick," Jack says, opening the door and letting him inside.

Frederick smiles and looks around the room. His eyes settle on Lucy and me.

153

"Hi, Martha," Frederick says. "Smells like a slice of heaven in here."

"Bacon," Lucy says. "Many slices of bacon and they're delicious and mostly gone."

She stretches her free hand over and grabs another piece, shoving it in her mouth. She steps back behind me. Frederick laughs. He nods to Martha, who offers him a chair.

"Sit down, Frederick," she says. "I'll get you some coffee and a plate."

"Well, I'm here more for business than pleasure, unfortunately," he says.

The hairs on my arms stand up. I knew it. This is not a social call.

"Now, Frederick," Jack says. "I told you some things this morning as a friend, not as a police officer."

"I'm aware of that, Jack," he says, "but when I went to the station afterward, I did some checking to see if anything had been reported."

"What?" Martha steps up and asks.

"Early last evening, two girls were reported missing from their home on Float Avenue," he says. "And along with a missing person's report was a report of theft of an undisclosed amount of cash and some personal property."

"We don't have the cash," I say, knowing it was partly a lie but kind of the truth, since it had been stolen. "And any personal property we have is our own. You can't make us go back to that house ever. My Mama's boyfriend Danny is a sick pervert. He tried to abuse me and if you send us back there, it will be worse."

"So you are the girls we're looking for then?"

I don't say a word. Lucy hides further behind me. Figures that damn stupid Danny calls the cops and reports us. One day I hope Karma bites him square and fair.

"Now, Frederick," Jack says. "Let's discuss this situation over coffee. Please, sit. These girls have been through some traumatizing stuff."

154

"I'd like to, Jack," he says. "Let's just take the girls down to the station. I'm sure we can get this cleared up in no time. You and Martha can join them if you'd like."

Martha sighs and looks over at Jack. Jack looks at Lucy and me apologetically.

"Better get your stuff girls," he says. "I am so sorry. I never meant for this to happen. We know your story and we'll go with you. We are here for you."

Jack turns toward Frederick. "I'm sure if you'd just listen to the whole story, you'd leave here and pretend you never saw them."

"I could lose my job, Jack," he says. "If the report hadn't been filed, it might be a different story."

"I'll help you get your things," Martha says.

"No, that's ok," I say. "We'll get them. We need to use the bathroom. We'll be right out."

I turn and walk toward our room. Lucy follows, bewildered at the turn of events. Once inside the room, I whisper to her.

"There is no way in hell we're going with that cop to the police station. They'll either call DCFS and separate us, or call Danny and Mama and tell them to come get us. Neither one is an option."

"What are we going to do?" Lucy asks.

All I want is for Lucy and I to have a normal life, to have someone love us enough to want to take care of us. Why is that so hard? Damn Danny. Damn Mama. Damn Jack for telling Frederick. Damn Daddy for letting his weakness win.

"Cart," Lucy says again, shaking me. "What are we going to do?"

"We're going to make a run for it," I say.

"How?" she asks.

"You girls ok?" Martha calls from the kitchen.

"Yes," I say. "Just getting our stuff and going to the bathroom."

I turn back to Lucy. "Grab your bag and follow me."

Once in the bathroom, I shut and lock the door behind us. I turn to the window, which faces the back of the house and slide up the screen. I throw my backpack out, then Lucy's.

"Come here. We need to move fast," I say.

Lucy moves next to me. I flush the toilet to muffle the sound of me lifting her up and out of the window. She slides through easily and is standing on the grass outside in an instant. Thank God for first floor bathrooms with windows. I flush one more time, and then lift myself up and out of the window.

"We're going to run as fast as we can," I say, "and make our way toward the park. There's lots of hiding places there."

"Then what?" Lucy says.

"I don't know," I say. "All I know is we are not going to the police station, we're not going back to Danny and Mama and we are not getting separated. Maybe we can come back here when the coast is clear."

Lucy and I pick up our backpacks, place them securely on our backs, and run like hell.

29

We cut through yards, only slowing down to check the streets for cops, or Jack and Martha. We stop beside a house to catch our breath, and hear a deep bark, followed by a low and rumbling growl. Crap. It sounds like a large dog, who is not happy to have us near his yard. We can't risk getting caught. Sucking in a deep breath, we continue running. It's so hot. And our bellies are full from breakfast. Not great running conditions.

By now, everyone must be aware we cut out through the bathroom window. Frederick has probably called for back up. I wonder how many cops there are in Freeport. I honestly don't care if we're in more trouble now than before. Any punishment the cops dole out won't hold a candle to what Danny will do. We have no choice but to run. I can't risk us getting separated. We will stick together come hell or high water.

"Cart," Lucy says, gasping for air. "I'm tired. Can't we stop somewhere and catch our breath?"

Lucy stops, her chest heaving. Sweat from the hot, morning sun, drips down and burns her eyes. She rubs them endlessly. Her poor little face is splotched red. She needs water. So do I.

"Ok," I say. "We'll stop here for a minute and then we have to get going. We need to find somewhere safe to hide out. It's not going to get dark for a long time."

"I'm not sure I want it to get dark," Lucy says, stopping between two houses.

"I know, but we won't be spotted as easily once it's dark," I add.

I see a faucet on the side of one of the houses, like before. Whoever thought of water faucets on the outside of a house was a genius. We turn the water on, get our fill and splash our faces.

We don't speak, but I know a thousand things are churning in each of our heads. I wish I was either a little kid, with my daddy still here, or maybe even a grown adult, living on my own, not answering to Mama or anyone. Honestly, whichever one would get us out of our life at this moment would be fine with me.

"We should keep moving," I finally say.

"I know," Lucy replies.

Her expression is so sad. I don't know what to do to make this better.

"I wish we had my Magic 8 Ball," I say.

"What would you ask it that we'd want to know the answer to?" Lucy asks.

She has a point.

"I could ask it if our splotchy red faces are going to explode from running in the heat!" I say with a laugh.

"It would say, *Signs Point To Yes*," Lucy says, fanning her face.

"Well, that could be ugly," I say with a smile.

Lucy laughs. We start out walking instead of running, just in case. We are careful to watch for approaching cars. As we near the front entrance to the park, we decide it's too open for there to be any good hiding places. We need to be able to crouch behind something ASAP, in case the cops, Jack and Martha, or Danny show up. We decide to take the long way around and come in the back entrance. I don't like going this way. We did it once, and discovered there's an old, rickety bridge you have to cross to get into the park. It's one of those old, metal bridges with open metal floor grates. It's scary walking across while looking down at the water rushing below.

Lucy and I grab each others hand, hold our breath and walk across as fast as we can. Once inside the park, we head over to a shaded area out of the way and make a plan. We sit down behind the trunk of a large tree, away from the road.

"This isn't going to be easy," Lucy says. "Now we have to hide from the cops, Mama, Danny, Martha and Jack. The list keeps getting longer and longer."

"All of that," I say, "for two girls who only want to be loved." Immediately, I regret saying that. "We don't need any of them. We are family and we love each other. That's all we need. Maybe we'll find Daddy and maybe we'll find his mama. We have nothing if we don't have hope. We have to believe we aren't going to have a crappy life forever."

"I want to believe you, Cart," Lucy says.

We crouch down when we hear an approaching car. I'm glad we picked a wide tree to hide behind. No one can possibly see us from the road. Just the same, I peek out from behind the tree.

"It's a park police car," I say.

"Can he see you?" Lucy asks.

"I don't think so."

The car slows down near the tree and I pull my head back. I look around for a place to run to in case he gets out of his car. Could we toss ourselves into the bushes along the river?

If there is such a thing as guardian angels, one could help us out any time. Lucy and I hold our breath and don't move a muscle. Thankfully, we hear the car move past us and head down the road.

"It this what it's going to be like?" Lucy asks. "Being afraid every time we hear a car or see people?"

"Until we figure out what we're doing, maybe," I say.

"Well, how long can we go on like that?"

"Probably not very long," I say. "I still have the phone book page in my pocket with the address of what could be Daddy's mama's house. Do you want to try and find it?"

"Might as well," Lucy says. "Where is it?"

I reach in my pocket and pull out the phone book page. I look at the address.

"It's not far from here," I say. "It's inside the park entrance. Do we risk walking there now in the middle of the day?"

"Is there another way to get there, where we won't be seen?" Lucy asks.

"Umm, if we swim through the creek over there and climb straight up that bluff, maybe," I say, pointing.

"Nice, Cart," Lucy says.

We both laugh.

"Maybe we should wait until dusk," I say. "That's only seven hours from now."

"What do we do until then?" Lucy asks.

"Will anybody besides the cops, Mama, Danny, Martha and Jack think anything of two girls playing in the park on a warm, sunny day?" I ask.

"Carrying heavy backpacks with our life in it won't be too noticeable either on a hot day," Lucy says.

My sarcasm has apparently rubbed off. I chuckle.

"Where *did* you get that attitude?" I ask and laugh.

"Only from the best," Lucy responds.

"I don't know about you, but I could use a nap," I say. "Let's just hang out here for a while and maybe sleep a bit. It's pretty quiet over here. Everyone seems to be over by the slides, Merry-Go-Round and other playground equipment."

Lucy and I slide down behind the trunk and use our backpacks as pillows. It doesn't take long for me to sink into a semi-restless sleep. I dream of Daddy.

30

This is the place, I tell Lucy. The walkway winding toward the large, wooden entrance is paved in oversized river stones. Colorful flowers line the pathway. The sun is shining on the front of the upscale, brick house, giving it a fresh and friendly feel. I am confident my daddy is inside. Lucy huddles close behind me as we approach the front door. I ring the bell and hear shuffling on the other side. The knob jiggles and the door opens. A man answers. His hair is cut short to his head except for a long and crazy beard on his chin, which reaches down to his chest. He has more lines contouring his face than I remember, but there is no doubt in my mind. That's my daddy. He stands there for a brief moment, furrowing his brow, trying to figure out if I'm real or a dream. A smile fills his entire face and he screams Cart, Baby, it's you! It's really you! I've been looking everywhere for you, and for such a long time. You found me. I've dreamed of this day. He picks me up in his arms and swings me around full circle, laughing and kissing my cheeks. I can't believe I've finally found you...Cart....Cart....Cart...

"Cart, Cart, Cart."

I shake the sleep from my head and sit up in a panic. Lucy is pushing on my shoulder, yelling my name over and over.

"What? What is it?" I scream. "Has somebody found us? Do we need to run?"

"Cart," Lucy says. "No one has found us. I have to pee."

"You are kidding me," I say, sitting back down, taking deep breaths to calm my heart, which is this side of popping out of my chest. "How long was I asleep?"

"I don't know," Lucy says, "maybe a couple of hours."

"Did you sleep at all?" I ask.

"Yes, until I woke up because I have to pee. I thought you might get mad at me if you woke up and I had wandered off without you."

"Good call. I would have panicked for sure," I say.

"See then?" she says. "It wasn't such a bad thing that I scared the crap out of you. It's better than the alternative."

"I'm beginning to think I'm teaching you far too much," I say with a giggle. "Let's head over to the bathrooms."

Lucy and I stuff our backpacks into the bushes in front us, safe from anyone walking by, but not too far in that we shove them into the river on the other side. Like Lucy says, we'll look a lot less suspicious if we aren't lugging them around on a hot summer day.

We peek out from behind the tree and look around. No cops, no Danny or Mama and no Jack and Martha lurking around, so we make our way past the duck pond toward the bathroom.

"What were you dreaming about?" Lucy asks. "I think you were happy. You were laughing and crying while you slept. You're kind of weird, Cart."

I laugh. "I'm sure of that," I say. "I was dreaming that we went to Daddy's mama's house and he was there and was happy to see us."

"Are we still going there later today?" Lucy asks.

"I'm getting tired of disappointment," I say, "but we need to either start making discoveries or crossing dead ends off of our list."

"I vote for making discoveries," Lucy says.

"This is a good discovery," I say, pointing to the brick building just on the other side of the dirt path.

"A bathroom," Lucy says with a smile, "and just in time."

Once we get back outside, we look around the park. There are a few moms and dads sitting on benches near their children, who are playing on the slides, teeter totters and in the sand. We see some people on the boats, over by the place we danced to the Merry-Go-Round music. That was a fun day. It's weird sometimes, how things can change in a short time. Life takes you places you'd never dream possible. And there's probably a good reason for that. It sucks.

Lucy and I sit at a picnic table near some people and try to blend in. We stay away from the roads and the cars that might be traveling through the park looking for two girls.

At least with Danny, we'll hear him coming from a long way away. Cops are also easy enough to spot. Wish I knew what Jack and Martha drive. For some reason they don't worry me as much. I think they'd still have our back. I'm sure they felt terrible about what happened. It's too risky to go back there right now. I bet the cops will be checking in on them to see if we've been in contact. They don't strike me as the type to lie and would feel obligated to tell if we were there. Maybe if it gets too bad out here we can go back there. I'd like to think they'd help us.

"What are we going to do about school?" Lucy asks.

"School?" I say. "We have a lot of time to worry about that. It doesn't start for at least another month or so."

"Who's going to sign us up?" she asks. "How are we going to get supplies and clothes and lunch money?"

"I hate that all of this has turned you into such a worrier," I say. "We'll figure it out. I promise I will always take care of you and figure out a way to keep you safe."

"I know you will, Cart," Lucy says. "You have so far."

Lucy reaches over and hugs me. Tears burn my eyes. I know far too well how someone can feel happy and sad at the same time. Lucy leans back and looks around, hoping our display of affection hasn't drawn attention. No one sees us. No one ever sees us.

"I'm hungry," Lucy says.

"How can that be?" I say. "You had enough bacon this morning to keep a grown man full for at least a day."

Lucy and I both laugh.

"What can I say?" she says.

"Ok, let's get to our backpacks and make some peanut butter sandwiches," I say.

Lucy and I make our way back to our new home-away-from-home. Everything is just as we left it. After eating, we kick back against the trunk of the tree and think about tonight. We decide to hang outside of Daddy's mama's house and watch from a distance behind a tree and see if we can see anyone inside. We need to make sure cops aren't coming around checking up. I don't know how much they know about us, or if they know anything about Daddy or his mama. Better safe than sorry. I don't want to be trapped inside.

Before we know it, dusk has settled across the skies. The beautiful reds of the setting sun have been replaced by impending darkness. It's a mixture of happiness and fear. We're happy to be able to move around more freely, yet are afraid of being outside at night. All night. Alone. We don't know what lurks around after dark. Hopefully nothing, or no one.

"How far away is her house?" Lucy asks.

"A short way up the main road that leads out of the park," I say.

"We're taking the road?" Lucy asks.

"We can't swim across the river to get there," I say.

Lucy becomes quiet.

"It'll be ok," I say. "Just stay close to me and be prepared to run. There are lots of trees to keep us hidden along the way."

We grab our backpacks and head out. Taking the winding path along the river, we cross the foot bridge, pausing for a minute to look down at the rushing water below. It flows freely across the smooth, wet rocks. The water occasionally jumps up and sprays a mist that reaches our faces. Its feels cool after a dry, hot day. Between the rushing water and getting lost in the sweetness of the water spraying us, we don't notice the car that pulls up nearby, until the lights flash red and blue. The officer shines a spotlight on our faces.

"Oh, no," I scream, looking right into the blinding lights. "Run, Lucy!"

31

"Hey," the cop yells, keeping his light trained on us. "Stay there."

Yeah, that's not going to happen. We are not getting caught. I pause for a brief moment, wondering if he will shoot. It's a chance we'll have to take. I grab Lucy's hand as we hurry to get off the bridge, away from the bright light. It almost feels as if we're stuck in that one spot, running and running, but not getting traction to move into the darkness.

Finally, in what seems like hours, we clear the bridge and duck into a nearby thick of trees on the other side. We stop behind a wide tree, panting, trying to catch our breath while listening for footsteps, gun shots, or any noise that'll let us know if he's nearby.

We see the spotlight flashing around the trees in the distance, waiting to settle on movement. Our movement. I can vaguely hear him talk into his walkie-talkie. Is he calling for back up? We must be in a lot of trouble. Now more than ever, we can't get caught. And if we stay in this spot, we will get caught. I motion for Lucy to continue running. We zigzag through the trees, up toward the road, which I think should have us coming out not too far from the connecting road that leads to Daddy's mama. It's almost completely dark and if we don't get out of these trees soon, I'm afraid we're going to get lost in them.

"Cart," Lucy says, as we run. "What's going to happen to us if we get caught? Will they separate us?"

"We're not going to find out," I say. "We are not going to get caught. I will never allow anyone to separate us. Ever. Okay?"

Lucy nods, as we continue our way through the woods. I can tell even in the darkness, she's not sure if I can deliver. Turning back towards the path ahead of us, it looks a bit lighter. As we get closer, we see it's the edge of the woods. Lucy and I stop short of exiting. I wipe the sweat from my face. It stings my eyes. Even though it's getting dark, it's still hot. I wish we had water to drink and cool off with. I guess I'd still take the heat over the freezing cold. I wouldn't mind it being cold long enough to kill off these mosquitoes though. They are eating us alive.

"Now what?" Lucy asks.

"Looks like the tree line follows the road a while longer," I say. "We'll stay on this side of the trees and follow it, so we're ready to duck back inside if we see lights."

My plan works great until a short distance later, we run into a wire fence, which blocks our path. It must be the start of someone's yard and the end of park property. We'll have to take the road. We stop and listen for any noise or approaching lights. Nothing. Good.

Lucy and I take off running. The street we're looking for is up ahead. We get to about fifty feet from making the turn and we see lights coming at us from ahead. We stop in our tracks. I turn, ready to head back to where we just left, only to find lights coming up the hill behind us as well. Neither light has settled on us yet.

"Run!" I yell to Lucy, who is already ahead of me and is pulling on my hand, moving me along.

It must be the cop coming up behind us and there's no mistaking the car that's ahead of us. Danny. What in the hell is he doing coming to the park? It creeps me out to think he hangs out in the park after dark. Pervert. It wouldn't surprise me. Or, maybe he knows we've been spotted at the park and he's coming to find us. I shiver at the thought.

Lucy and I reach the street and turn the corner as Danny's car lights come up over the hill, shining on the spot we were just standing. My stomach lurches at the sight of him. I could have lived my entire life without ever seeing or hearing his car ever again. The car from the park comes into view. It's the cop. He's shining his flood light out of the car window, moving at a snail's pace. Lucy and I dive into the nearby bushes and watch. I'm sure no one has seen us. Danny's car slows down when he sees the cop. He must be looking for us. We duck down low when the light shines in our direction. Danny's car comes to a stop. If the cop finds us, will Danny try to make us go with him? Will the cop let him? Lucy cries. I'll admit the thought of getting caught here and now is too overwhelming. I shush Lucy.

Danny gets out of his car and waves at the cop, who stops and gets out of his car. I wish I knew what they were saying. I'm pretty sure it's about us. We're too far away to hear, but I have a good idea. Danny probably told the cop he is our loving stepdad and wants us to be safe and to come back home. He's probably telling the cop he'd be willing to overlook the fact that we stole from him. I roll my eyes thinking of the lies that are spilling from his disgusting mouth.

Next thing I see, the cop is gesturing with his hand toward the park, then pointing at the trees behind him and looking toward our direction. Great. Now Danny *knows* we've been spotted in this area. He and the cop will be cruising around the park until we get caught.

I look over at Lucy. Tears stain her sweaty face but she's silent. She's hugging her backpack. If it were a balloon, it would have exploded by now. The look on her face makes me more determined than ever not to get caught. I need to figure out how we can get out of this once and for all. I want to find our daddy, but what if he's as screwed up as everyone else in our life? Jack and Martha are our best bet at a normal life. I wonder what the odds are of them wanting to take care of us. I envy her children and grandchildren. I hope they appreciate the love I'm sure they've felt all of their lives.

Lucy shakes my arm as a car door slamming jolts me back to the here and now. Danny gets back into his car and revs up the engine. He heads into the park. The cop continues lighting the roadside with his flood light, then turns around and heads back into the park, too. Good. Maybe they think we're still in the woods, or in the park hiding out somewhere.

"Now what do we do?" Lucy asks.

"I don't know. See if we can find Daddy's mama's house. It should be up the road a few houses, if it's even her that lives there. Our track record hasn't been great so far."

"That's for sure," Lucy says.

It's quiet now except for the sound of Danny's car in the distance. I can tell he's still driving around the park. I'm glad we can hear him this far away, but he's still too close. I wonder what Mama is doing. I wonder why she wasn't out with Danny searching. I bet Danny wanted to find us first, without Mama. That way, he could threaten us or hurt us without Mama seeing anything. He's such a creep. Lucy and I stay put a bit longer. We're both too scared to leave the safety of the bushes.

"Are we going to knock on her door?" Lucy asks.

"I don't know," I answer.

"Are we going to sleep outside?" she asks.

"I don't know," I answer.

"What if she's just as awful as Daddy has always said," she asks.

"That's what I'm afraid of," I answer.

32

I'm not sure how much time has passed. I don't hear
Danny's car anymore. I don't know if that's good or bad.
We're still sitting in the bushes. Oddly, I feel safe here. It's
completely dark and kind of scary outside, but in here, it's
like our own little world that no one knows about. The only
time Lucy and I have been outside in the dark has been in
our own yard catching lightning bugs. I think back to one of
the last times Daddy, Lucy and I caught lightning bugs
together. Lucy was a baby, crawling, but not walking.

~

"Hey Cart, baby," Daddy says laughing. "They're all
lighting up over here. You're missing them."

A big, dramatic sigh escapes my mouth and Daddy
laughs. I run over to him and stop right next to him and
watch. Sure enough, one lights up by his leg. I swoop my
hand over it while it's still lit up and close my fingers around
it. I unfold them to see if I caught it. I peer inside my cupped
hand.

"I caught it, Daddy," I yell, jumping up and down, closing
my fist tight again.

"I knew you could," Daddy says. "Now, let's not squeeze it so hard you smash the little fella before we get it in the jar."

Daddy brings over the glass peanut butter jar that I watched him wash out and clean this morning. He had poked holes in the metal lid with a screw driver and a hammer so any lightning bugs we catch could breathe while inside the jar. He let me tap on the screw driver with the hammer a few times. It was so heavy, I almost dropped it. Lucy helped me pull grass and throw it into the bottom of the jar.

Daddy said we could keep the bugs in the jar until we go inside for bed but then we have to release them. He said it wouldn't be fair to let them die in the jar. He said no one wants to die in captivity.

"I want to keep them, Daddy," I say, "but I don't want them to die. We'll let them go."

"Thatta girl, Cart," Daddy says and hugs me. "You're a good little trooper."

I open my clenched fist as he takes the lid off the jar. I shake the bug. It slides out of my hand and falls onto the soft grass inside the jar, lighting up when it lands. Daddy screws the lid back on before it flies up and out. Lucy giggles and points at the bug in the jar, who is amusing her with its light show. Daddy sets it in the grass next to Lucy as I run off in search of more.

By the time Mama comes out and tells us it's time for bed, we have caught ten lightning bugs. Lucy sits on Daddy's lap, and I crowd in next to him. We sit in the grass, peering inside the jar, mesmerized by the lights flashing on and off. We feel sad when Mama says we have to go to bed. That means we have to let them go. Mama always ruins our fun.

"It's cool," Daddy says, wiping a tear from my eye. "We can catch more tomorrow night, Cart. That's the beauty of summer. There are lightning bugs almost every night."

171

~

"Cart," Lucy says, nudging my arm and bringing me out of my sweet memory.

"Sorry, Lucy," I say. "I was thinking about the time Daddy and I were catching lightning bugs. You were a baby. You helped by throwing grass into the jar and everywhere else!"

"I wish I could remember that, or anything about Daddy," Lucy says. "I can't."

Lucy and I look out into the darkness from the safety of the bushes. Lightning bugs begin to light up the night. They only come in the summer time and only in certain areas of the country. I'm glad we are in one of those areas. It's almost magical to watch them sparkle and shine in the night.

"Sounds pretty quiet out there," I say. "Should we see what we can find at Daddy's mama's, *if* she really is his mama?"

"I guess," Lucy says. "How come we don't call her Grandma?"

"I don't know. I think the title of grandma should be for someone who has earned it," I say. "She hasn't earned it yet, or maybe never will. As far as that goes, Mama doesn't deserve to be called Mama either."

"That's a true story," Lucy says.

"And it'll be a cold day in hell before we call Danny, Daddy," Lucy and I say in unison.

We both laugh hysterically. Funny how we think the same exact thing sometimes.

"I'm sure Mama would slap me for teaching you to say that," I say with a smile. "Yet, it's the truth. She'd be the first to say it herself. Alright, let's go check this out," I say.

Lucy takes a deep breath and I can feel her eyes on me, even in the dark.

"Ok, whatever happens, we have each other," she says.

"Always," I respond.

Lucy and I crawl out of the bushes, dragging our backpacks behind us. Our legs have fallen asleep and feel numb and unsteady. As we shake them off and start moving toward the house, someone steps out of the shadows and blocks our way.

"What are you two doing out here in the dark?" a male voice asks.

My mind is racing through a hundred scenes faster than I can process them. Who is he? Do I play it cool? Do I recognize his voice? Is he going to try to hurt us? Can I kick him or hurt him so we can get away? I pull Lucy behind me, making sure she's out of his reach. She's almost completely stiff, like a statue.

"Um, we're going to our grandma's," I say, my voice shaking. I'm sure I wasn't anywhere near convincing.

"Who is your grandma?" he asks. "And what respectable grandma lets her grandchildren roam the streets at night without supervision?"

He's got me there. What respectable parent anywhere lets their children roam the streets at night? The short answer is they don't.

"Eleanor Matthews," I spit out, almost wishing I'd have made a name up, then getting mad at myself for telling him anything. We don't owe him any kind of explanation. He steps closer and the light from the street corner shines on him. I don't know him. He must see the fear on our faces and his face softens.

"There are lots of weird people that come out at night," he says. "Two young girls shouldn't be out alone."

You're telling me, I think to myself. Maybe, I'm finally learning that my smart mouth shouldn't be for everyone to hear.

"We're just heading a few houses that way," I point.

"Well, I wouldn't be able to rest tonight if I didn't make sure you made it there safe and sound."

Great. I think. I silently wonder if we shouldn't just kick him and run anyway, except I stupidly gave him Eleanor's name. Not that it really matters; she doesn't know us from a hill of beans.

"Really, sir," I say. "We'll be fine. It's just three houses up."

"Well, let's get a move on it then," he says. "I'm sure your grandma is getting tired and about ready for bed. What's the address?"

Resigned to the fact that he's not going away, I tell him 1110. We begin walking in that direction. He shines his small penlight on the mailboxes. It reminds me of Danny's penlight and my searching in his closet, finding all of that money. Then, the homeless man taking it, along with my Magic 8 Ball. I'd give anything to be able to shake it now and ask it what to do. I'm sure it would give me the same ridiculous answers it always has like, *Ask Again Later* or *Reply Hazy, Try Again.* But you never know, maybe I'd shake it up good and peek inside and it'd finally say something positive or helpful like, *Outlook Good.*

We are now standing in front of Eleanor Matthews' house. Our new friend doesn't send us on our merry way to the door. Oh, no, he has to walk us up to the door and knock. This, after I repeatedly tell him we're fine and he can leave now. This is not how I want to meet Eleanor Matthews for the first time, especially if she is our grandmother. Why is it you get all the help in the world from people you don't need or want help from, but when you seriously need it, no one cares or is anywhere to be found. After a few minutes and another loud knocking, we hear footsteps on the other side. She is coming to the door. All of a sudden I feel light-headed and the urge to bolt becomes strong. The embarrassment that's possibly waiting is too much to bear. Will they call the cops and hold us until they get here because she'll say she has no clue who we are, and that we must be liars and thieves out on a scam?

The door opens. She stands there quietly looking at Lucy and me, and then over at our chaperone.

"Hello, Mrs. Matthews," he says. "Your granddaughters here were out walking alone in the dark and I thought it prudent they have a chaperone to make sure they get safely to you."

Oh, brother, I think. This is where it could get interesting. The look of surprise on her face is quite obvious. She mutters a thank you, along with a weak smile. He bids us a good evening and disappears into the dark. That's it? No scene?

I warily look at her and try to gauge her thoughts or next move, anything I can get from her body language and piercing stare. She stands there looking at us, not saying a word. It's obvious that she's our grandma. There is a definite resemblance to my daddy. Lucy moves behind me, as we all stand there gawking. I can't believe she hasn't slammed the door in our face. Then it dawns on me, that I also resemble my daddy and she must be able to see it too. Finally, she speaks.

"What are your names?" she asks gruffly.

I feel Lucy grabbing the back of my shirt, pulling it taut. I suck in a deep breath, to steady my voice.

"I'm Cart and she's Lucy," I say.

Lucy peeks out from behind me.

"Cart and Lucy, huh?" she says, looking us up and down. "No doubt for McCartney and Lucy as in *Lucy in the Sky with Diamonds*, right?"

"That's what Daddy always told me," I say with a smile.

Without missing a beat or with even a tiny touch of friendliness, she asks, "What do you want?"

My smile disappears. What do we want? I hadn't thought beyond wanting someone to actually give a crap about us. The only person I knew ever did was my daddy, her son. Apparently, it stopped there. I look up into her cold, hard face. No welcoming smile. No impending hug. No I'm happy you're here, come inside so we can catch up on the last fifteen years of your life. I'm sure I had a stupid look on my face. She stood at the door, impatiently waiting for my response.

33

"We're trying to find our daddy," I say. "Is he still alive? Do you know where he is?"

She stares at us a moment longer before answering.

"I don't know where your daddy is. Last I knew he was still alive."

I feel a glimmer of hope but also sadness. What's with these parents who don't know or care where their children are or what they're doing? Even when they're grown adults, they should know. I hope one day when I have kids that I will love them and be there for them no matter what. Always.

"Where was he last living?" I ask.

"Here in Freeport," she says. "He's not the daddy you remember him to be."

Confused, I look at Lucy, then back at her.

"What does that mean?"

"It means your daddy is a no-good loser. Just like his own loser dad."

My daddy has never spoken about his dad, at least not that I can remember. I wonder why that is, now that I think about it, but I'm not going to ask her.

"My daddy is not a no-good loser," I yell at the wretched woman who is my grandmother. "He's my daddy and I love him. I know he loves us. We want to find him. I know he's been trying to find us. You're just a mean, old lady. He's always told me you've never loved him, or anybody else for that matter."

She nodded, but it wasn't because she agreed with what I said.

"I see you have a lot of Jack's defiance and smart mouth in you. Bet it's gotten you into your fair share of trouble over the years, hasn't it?"

I cross my arms and stare at her.

"Just as I figured," she says, crossing her arms and smirking, like she thinks she knows me. "Why are you both carrying backpacks and roaming the streets after dark?"

"It doesn't matter," I say.

"You came knocking on my door. Are you runaways?" she asks.

I'm not about to tell her anything. I'm not giving her a chance to call the cops and tell them two runaway girls knocked on her door. They already know we're in this area. If they catch us, I know they'll split us up. I'm not going to let that happen.

"No," I answer. "We're just looking for our daddy."

"Well, he's not here," she says. "Where's your good for nothing mother? She's on to the next flavor-of-the-week boyfriend, no doubt."

I couldn't argue with that. Clearly, she's met my mama.

"She's here in Freeport," I say.

"Oh, I know she is," she answers. "She's already called me up looking for money."

"Money?" I ask. "She knows you live here?"

"She's been hounding me for money for as long as I can remember. I figured it was a matter of time before her children came knocking on my door looking for the same."

178

"What?" I say, surprised at her comment. "We don't want your damn money. All we've ever wanted is for somebody to love us and take care of us like our daddy did. I guess nobody like that exists. He was the best daddy in the world. Mama and the war screwed that up. Daddy used to come looking for us, but he hasn't for a long time. You were our last hope in finding him. But it turns out you're no different than any of the other crappy adults in our life. I should have expected that."

"You clearly got your smart mouth from both of your parents," she says. "I'm not surprised no one has ever taught you respect. Your mother wouldn't know it if it slapped her on the face."

"You don't have to worry about my smart mouth or us trying to get your precious money, or anything else from you," I say. "Thanks for nothing."

"Your daddy can't do nothing for you, anyway," she says.

I don't know what to say to that. I want to know why, but I'm too angry. I'm not about to ask. I grab Lucy's hand and we storm off into the darkness. Tears flow freely down my face. I don't hide them from Lucy, but I can't look at her either. She hasn't said a single word through any of this. I don't turn around to see what the old witch is doing. She didn't call after us or follow.

I spot a garage not far from her house and Lucy and I duck behind it, out of sight from the road and her house. I let go of Lucy's hand and slink down to the ground and cry.

"It's ok," Lucy says, patting my back and trying to comfort me. "We will find him. She said he's still alive and he's in Freeport. How hard can it be?"

I wipe the tears off of my face onto my shirt sleeve.

"How can we possibly find him before everyone else finds us? The odds are stacked against us, Lucy, like they always are. I'm sure that old witch raced to the phone to call the cops. Mama and Danny are looking for us. So are Jack and Martha. And the cops. They've already spotted us in this area. I don't know where we can go to be safe. If Daddy's this close, why hasn't he come around? I was sure he must have died or moved far away. He's been within an hour of us all of this time, Lucy, and he never tried to find us. He could have if he wanted to, you know. Why would she say he can't do anything for us? Maybe he thinks we're not worth loving, like everybody else."

"I don't believe that," Lucy says. "Not for a minute."

The tears flow again. I feel so defeated. I sob loudly, not caring if anyone hears or if we get caught. What difference does it make now? The one person I thought in this whole world who truly loved us is just like all of the rest of them.

"Don't fall apart on me, Cart," Lucy says. "We can figure this out. Between the two of us, we can do anything."

I hug Lucy. I love her so much. If we never find another person to love us and take care of us, we know we will do that for each other until the day we die. I'm quiet again and sit on the hard ground, not letting go of Lucy, trying to get as much comfort and energy from her as I can. I smell rain in the air before I actually feel it on my skin. We have nowhere to stay and now it's going to rain. It starts as a light mist and slowly gets heavier and heavier. I see a bolt of lightning flash through the sky, followed by a crack of thunder. Lucy jumps in my arms. I feel her shaking.

"What are we going to do, Cart?" she asks. "We can't stay out here in the rain. Where can we go? I didn't see anywhere in the park we could hide and not get wet, other than the bathroom. I don't want to get trapped in the bathroom. Besides, there were a lot of spiders in there. I can't sleep with spiders, Cart."

One more thing I have to think about. My head throbs. I look around to see if there's something we can hide under to stay dry. It's so dark out it's hard to see. I notice a door on the side of the garage, not far from where we are sitting. I stand up and walk over to it. Lucy follows. I jiggle the knob.

It's unlocked. I push the door open. I wish I had Danny's penlight right about now.

Damn that stupid, homeless man. I'd sure like to find him again. I grab Lucy's hand and we step inside, closing the door behind us. We try to let our eyes to adjust to the darkness but it's not working. Fortunately, another flash of lightning shines through the garage window and we get a brief peek at our surroundings. I see a riding lawnmower and a bunch of junk cluttering up the corner. Garden tools hang on the wall. There's a car covered by a canvas tarp in the center of the garage.

It goes dark again. Lucy has the death grip on me as I make my way over to the car. I wish I knew how to drive; I'd pull the tarp off, open the garage door and drive as far away from this town and the crappy people in it as I could. Maybe we'd go someplace warm, so if we were homeless, at least we wouldn't freeze to death.

Instead, I feel around in the dark for car door handle under the tarp. I lift the tarp and open the door a crack. We sneak underneath and scoot inside. There is no back seat, just a front. It smells a little musty underneath the tarp. This car probably hasn't seen the light of day for a long time. I hope there's nothing else in here with us, like spiders or mice. I put it out of my head. I have no plans of mentioning it to Lucy. I'm sure she's thinking about it anyway.

"Cart," Lucy says. "It stinks in here."

"I know," I say. "It's a little musty."

"If I feel one thing crawl on me," she says, "I'm out of here."

"I know how you feel," I say, "but we need a dry and somewhat comfortable place to sleep tonight and this looks like it's going to be our only option."

I put my backpack against the driver's door to use as a pillow. Lucy puts hers on the floor and she snuggles in next to me. It's not the softest place, and it's definitely not too roomy, but it's better than being out in the rain or on the hard, cement of the garage or on the wet ground. I awake some hours later to Lucy shaking me.

"Cart," she says, trying to get me awake. "I have to go to the bathroom."

"Oh, Lucy," I say, "can't we sleep a little longer?"

"I'd go outside by myself, but I'm afraid," she says.

I could tell by her voice that she meant business. I stretch myself awake and we grab our backpacks and sneak out from under the tarp. I can see from the garage window that it must be early morning. It's barely starting to get light outside. This is probably as good of time as any to get out of here. The rain must have stopped some time during the night, and all is quiet except for a few early morning birds. I open the side door of the garage, peek out and look around. The coast looks clear.

We head down the street toward the park and bathrooms. It's too early for anybody to be out and about, so I feel fairly safe. Even so, we stay close to the tree line in case we have to slip inside to hide. It's dark enough that a car coming would have their lights on, so we'll see them coming. We hear a rustling in the woods near us and freeze in place. A mama deer and her two babies enter the grassy area in front of us. Their ears perk when they see and smell us. The mama herds them back into the woods to safety. Lucy and I smile.

A few minutes later, we're back in the park, making a beeline for the bathroom. We look around to make sure no one sees us. It's still fairly dark. Besides, who gets up this early? We go inside and take care of business, then wash up a bit. Sitting in the far corner, clear from the spiders, we make ourselves peanut butter sandwiches, relishing the feeling of eating something again. The peanut butter makes us thirsty and we use the sink to get a drink from the faucet. We cup our hands to hold the water. It's messy, but it works.

Finally, we change our clothes and brush our hair and teeth, shoving everything back in our backpacks when we're done.

A twig snapping outside of the bathroom entrance gets our attention. I put my finger to my mouth and motion for Lucy to move over to the corner with me. Another twig snaps. Someone is out there. It's hardly morning yet, who would be up this early? Joggers? Maybe our imaginations are running crazy and it's either nothing or an animal, like a raccoon.

Then I hear it. Footsteps. Unmistakable footsteps. My chest hurts. I push Lucy behind me. We are extra quiet and still, as Danny enters the bathroom.

34

"I knew you'd come back here eventually," he says. "The cop told me you were spotted in the area. Of course, he thinks I'm the next best thing since sliced bread and your safety and return home is my only concern."

Oh, officer, I know they didn't mean to steal from me. I didn't want to press charges. Their mother believes in tough love. You know how teenagers try to be independent and make bad choices. They're good kids. They need some extra attention and understanding. I've been working so many overtime hours, it's my fault, really. I only want them home.

I don't know what to say. Words won't come out. Lucy is sobbing behind me. I feel trapped. I'm sure it shows on my face.

"What's the matter, Cart?" he asks. "Cat got your tongue? Poor Cart. You think you're so damn smart, but you are no match for me."

"We didn't hear your car," I finally spit out.

"Of course you didn't," he answers, feeling confident and smart. "It's parked at the other end of the lot. I've been waiting here for you all night. The kind police officer told me I could stay here, even though the park closes at 10:30. He knows how worried I've been for your safe return. I knew eventually you'd make yourselves seen. You're too sissified to pee outside."

"What do you want, Danny?" I ask. "You don't want us around. Here's your chance to walk away and never hear from us again."

He moves closer to Lucy and me. Deliberately taking each step slowly, measured and calculated. Intimidating. He knows we're cornered and he's enjoying every minute of it.

"Oh, I think you know what I want, aside from that wad of cash you stole. And I'm going to get it," he says. "If this wasn't a public place, I'd take what I want right now, but I want to savor every minute, privately, with no interruptions or intrusions."

Lucy cries out. A sick feeling takes over me.

"You're both going to move back home and do my cooking and cleaning and anything else I want you to do. Anything. Do you understand? I think we know how useless June is. I see now it's been you two that must have done all of the work. June hasn't lifted a finger since you left two days ago."

"Mama may be a lot of things, but she won't let you hurt us," I say.

"June doesn't give a shit about anyone but herself," he says. "You don't see her out looking for you, do you? As long as someone pays her way and she can sit on her ass reading her magazines and drink beer, she doesn't care."

I can't really argue with that, but I'd like to think Mama wouldn't let him abuse us. I take a good, hard look at Danny. What is Mama thinking? His greasy, long hair and bushy sideburns are nasty. His Adam's Apple sticks out as he tips his head back in laughter. He's so smug. I won't let him see me cry.

"You can go straight to hell," I say. "I'll never do anything you say."

"Oh, yeah?" he says. "I bet your stupid little sister will. She can't fight me off and, quite frankly, neither can you."

"You leave Lucy alone," I say, narrowing my eyes. "Or I'll kill you."

His empty, condescending laugh pierces me like a knife.

"You aren't going to do shit."

He moves closer to Lucy. I lunge towards him without thinking. I start kicking and hitting him, screaming how I hate him and how one day he'll get what's coming to him.

He hits me in the mouth and then comes around with a punch that lands on my cheek. I fall to the ground. I can taste blood. Lucy screams and comes to me, but he grabs her. While I'm down he kicks me in the stomach. Air leaves my lungs and I gasp, overwhelmed by pain.

"You are more trouble than you're worth," I barely hear him say. "I will deal with you later. Right now, your little sister and I are going to take a drive."

He kicks me one more time, apparently for good measure and to make sure I stay down. I don't think my moving is going to be an issue. With blurred vision and a fog swirling in my head, I see him leaving with the one person I love the most in this world. Lucy is kicking him and screaming my name as he carries her out of the bathroom. I try to move and reach out to her but my body won't cooperate. I attempt to stand but sink back onto the hard, dirty cement floor and black out.

~

When I come to, I panic. I frantically look around. How long have I been out? I listen for Danny's car but don't hear anything. Are they still in the park?

"Lucy," I scream.

Pain racks my body as I stand. So this is what it feels like to get the crap kicked out of you. The pain in my stomach is unbearable. I take short, gaspy breaths, so it's less painful.

My mouth. Oh my God, my mouth! I stumble over to the mirror hanging behind the sink. I have a ginormous fat lip, purple and puffy, with a split in the middle of it. I reach my fingers up to touch it and wince. It's so painful. Crusting blood has dribbled down my chin. My cheek is red and puffy, too. I can see the indentation of his ring right in the middle of it. I smile to reveal my teeth. They are bloody, but all seem to be there and not loose.

I turn the faucet on, cup my hand and suck up the water as best I can. I swish it around in my mouth. It dribbles out of the puffy side onto my shirt. I spit what I can into the sink. I lift my shirt to inspect where he kicked me. It's red and bruising already. I can't touch it without wanting to sob.

I grab my backpack along with Lucy's. She must have dropped it when he scooped her up. I stagger out of the bathroom. It's much lighter now and the sun is shining. Already, it's going to be a hot day. How long have I been out? I listen for Danny's car. Nothing. Where would he have taken her? Home? Somewhere else?

I look around the parking lot in hopes they might still be here. No car. No one is around. No one can help. Figures. I have to somehow get to them before he hurts her. I'll never forgive myself if something happens to her.

I start walking. It's slow and pained. I have to make a plan. I realize the fastest way to get help is to go back to her, my grandma. I don't want to knock on her door again, but I have no choice. She's the closest person and I don't know how far I can walk. The saltiness of the tears burns my swollen lip.

It's only by the grace of God that I manage to reach her doorstep. My short breaths are quick and labored. I bang harshly on her door. I hear footsteps and then the door opens. She stands there looking at me. Words fail me.

"What in the Sam hell happened to you?" she asks. "Where is your sister?"

Surprisingly, she pulls me into her house and guides me to a chair. I sit down, flinching in pain as I do so.

"He has her," I say. "We have to hurry and find her before he hurts her. I don't know where he took her."

"Who has her?" she asks.

"Danny," I say.

"Who in the hell is Danny?"

"Mama's boyfriend."

"Did he do this to you?"

"Yes, then he stole Lucy."

"Is he living with your Mama?"

"Yes."

She walks over to her phone and dials 0 for an operator. She identifies herself as Eleanor Matthews and asks to be transferred to the police department. When they pick up, she tells them a man named Danny has assaulted one of her granddaughters and then, kidnapped the other one. She says Lucy is in danger and they need to immediately send a squad car to 1027 S. Float, where they may have headed. I'm surprised she knows the address. I wonder how she does.

She hangs up the phone and walks over to me. I start crying again. She's not a warm and fuzzy person and has no clue how to be of comfort. I'm not sure where my daddy learned it, but it wasn't from her. When Daddy comforted me, I felt like I was in a safe, warm cocoon.

"Will you take me there?" I ask. "Lucy needs me. We've never been apart. Please."

She pauses for a moment as she looks at me. I can't tell whether she hears the urgency in my voice or takes pity on my messed up face, but either way she agrees to drive me. She leads me through the kitchen to the side door and her waiting car.

The kitchen is small, but tidy, with avocado green cabinets, pale orange countertops and a metal table with pale orange vinyl seats. I like the orange and green together. Her floor is checker patterned in the same colors as the cabinets and counters, with a mix of cream tiles. It all looks brand new. I'm glad it's not yellow. I wonder if she hates yellow like I do. Maybe we have that in common. It's a good sign.

Her car is parked next to the side door, and I carefully ease myself into the passenger seat, tossing the backpacks in the space between us. I don't tell her about us sleeping in the car in the garage. Maybe it wasn't her garage.

We back down the driveway and head to Float Street. I'm so worried about Lucy. I pray Danny is all talk and no action and hasn't hurt her. Maybe he was saying those things to scare me. Is he really so creepy that he'd hurt her? She's eleven.

It seems like we hit every stoplight on the way. We pull up to the house the same time the police car does. I open the car door and get out faster than I should have, forgetting about my sore stomach. I look for Danny's car in his usual parking place. It's not there. My heart sinks. Where would he have taken her?

"Listen, young lady," the officer says, "You get back in the car until I can secure the area."

"His car isn't here," I cry, tears welling up in my eyes. "I don't know where else to look."

In a panic, I sprint through the yard toward the door, ignoring the officer and my pain. That's when I spot Danny's car parked around the corner in the alley. He never parks there.

"Lucy," I scream, running toward the house. I hope I'm not too late.

35

"Cart," I hear from inside the house. "Help me."

"Hold on, young lady," the cop says, grabbing me by the arm, stopping me in my tracks.

"Listen here," Eleanor says. "I'm her grandmother. You take your hands off of her."

"Let go of me," I say, breaking free. "He has my sister in there."

With great pain, I skip steps in order to get to the door faster. I push it open. It slams behind me. That's right, Danny. I am here. He's not too smart for leaving it unlocked. Did he think I would listen to him and not come find my sister? He's dumber than I thought.

The cop and Eleanor come in behind me, in time to see Danny pulling Lucy up out of the chair and pushing her toward the steps leading upstairs. Did he think he could hide her? She breaks free and runs to me.

"Cart," she sobs, as we embrace. I shrink back from the pain and she eases up on her hold.

"Are you ok?" I ask her. "Did he hurt you?"

"No," she says, "but he said terrible things to me, Cart. I was so scared he was going to hurt me. Are you ok? You look horrible. I thought he killed you. I'm so glad you're not dead. I was so afraid you were."

"I'll be fine," I say, and turn to Danny, "You bastard!"

I leave Lucy next to Eleanor and lunge at Danny, beating on his chest with both of my fists. My body screams in pain, but it feels good to pound the crap out of him, knowing he won't hit me back with an officer standing here. His lip twitches and his eyes grow dark. He holds up his hands as if to protect himself and reaches over and pinches me hard on the back of the arm. He briefly leans in closer.

"You will pay for this," he whispers in my ear.

"Young lady," the cop says, pulling me back, "Stop that this instant, or I'll arrest you for disorderly conduct."

I gently rub the back of my arm and glare over at Danny, who seems pleased with the pain he has secretly inflicted on me.

"Me? Disorderly conduct?" I ask. "How about him? He punched me in the face and kicked me in the stomach. And he just pinched the back of my arm."

I hold up my arm so everyone can see the angry, red mark emerging.

"I don't know what you're talking about, Cart," Danny says. "I have done nothing but try to be a good father figure to both of you girls. You attacked me. I didn't lay a hand on you. You are out of control and dangerous. I took Lucy away so you wouldn't hurt her."

"You're a liar," Lucy says.

Danny turns to Lucy and gives her a threatening look.

"See how you've corrupted your little sister with your lies, Cart?" he says turning back around. "She defends your horrible behavior. I'm sure it's due to fear."

"Fear? Of me? How do you explain this?" I say, pointing to my face.

"For all I know, you fell or did that to yourself and now you want to blame me for it," he says. "Officer, we talked last night. You know that I've been searching for these girls in order to bring them back home. Why would I try to harm them? I spent the entire night looking for them. Their mama and I plan to get married and they are part of the deal. We are going to become a family. A real family. They need a good daddy figure. Obviously, their own father is irresponsible and not in the picture. I only want to love them, like daughters. Their mama and I are here for them."

Eleanor coughs out loud, as if she's choking on the crap Danny's shoving down our throats. I'm glad she can see him for what he is. I hope the officer can see it, too.

Danny turns toward Eleanor and narrows his eyes. She does the same back at him. I don't think I'd want to make her mad and then have to deal with the consequences.

It's weird and cool at the same time to meet someone related to you, who you have never spent time with, and see you have similar traits. I don't want to like her, but I do. I push those thoughts to the back of my head. I can't handle another adult rejecting me, especially another family member.

"Well, you did seem quite sincere," the officer says.

"Then you're an idiot," I say to him.

"Young lady, you are pushing your luck," he replies.

"I see June knows how to pick winners," Eleanor says, eyeing Danny up and down.

"Ma'am, if you don't stay out of this, I'm going to have to arrest you for obstruction of justice."

"I'd like to see you go ahead and try," Eleanor says. "Doesn't take a rocket scientist to see he's full of shit."

She crosses her arms once again, over the top of her ample bosom, almost daring him to argue with her. Yep. There's definitely some genetics going on here between her, daddy and me. Even Lucy is starting to show signs of it.

"Just who in the hell are you?" Danny asks, looking at Eleanor.

"I will be your worst nightmare," Eleanor responds.

192

"Ain't that the damn truth," Mama says, entering the living room.

"Who are you?" the officer asks.

"I am these girls' Mama," she says. "What in the hell is going on here? Cart, who did that to your face? Did someone finally get tired of your smart mouth?"

"See, officer?" Danny says. "Even her own mama knows what she's like. It's truly a sad situation."

"Oh, brother," Eleanor says. "You and June here are the only truly sad things in the room."

Could Eleanor be sticking up for us? No one has ever stuck up for us besides Daddy.

"Mama," I say. "Danny did this and he stole Lucy from me and was going to hurt her just like I told you he tried to hurt me."

"Cart, I'm gonna slap you myself, if you don't stop telling those lies," Mama says, moving closer to me. "You need to stop trying to get attention by lying."

"Ma'am, I'm going to have to ask you to step back to where you were," the officer says.

The officer looks at each of us and says he's going to arrest the next person who moves or opens their mouth. He calls for backup.

"Yes," he says, "This is Officer Crump and I'm going to need a squad car to help bring a family in for questioning in a possible domestic abuse case. Yes, that's affirmative. Bring in a case worker from DCFS. Yes, there are two of them. One female approximately fifteen and another approximately eleven. Ok, see you shortly."

"DCFS?" Lucy cries. "You're bringing in DCFS? They're going to separate us, Cart. I'll never see you again. I'll run away before I'll come back here to live."

"We have to stay together," I say. "We're the only ones who have ever given a crap about each other. No one except our daddy ever cared about us. We need to find him. I know he'll take us so we can stay together."

"Cart, you don't know anything," Mama says.

"Hey, I told you not to make a move or say a word and I meant it," the officer says. "I'm taking everyone down to the station and we'll get each of your statements and figure out how to proceed from there."

We do as we're told this time, but there's a lot of mean faces and piercing eye stares. Not too long after, another cop arrives. Officer Crump takes Mama and Danny in his car and the second officer takes me, Lucy and Eleanor.

We arrive at the police station the same time as Mama and Danny. The officers guide us into the building and down a spotlessly clean hallway. Mama and Danny both stare at me, cold and hard. I look away and hold on to Lucy's hand as we walk.

I've never been in a police station before. I notice a door with a small window in it and peer inside as we march by. I see jail bars and panic. I wonder if he's going to arrest us and make us sit in one of those cells.

One by one, the officers put Mama, Danny and Eleanor in a room by themselves and shut the door behind them. I wonder if it's a cell with bars, but the doors shut too fast for me to see.

Now it's just me and Lucy. We squeeze each other's hand and a look of *I hope this isn't the last time I'll ever see you.*

36

The officer stops at an open door, as a lady stands up from her desk and smiles. She walks over.

"Hi," she says to both of us. "I'm Jessica Barnes. I'd like to ask you a few questions, if that's ok."

We don't answer back. If she's going to separate us, we don't want to be nice to her.

"I'm not here to hurt you in any way," she says. "But I do want to talk to each of you separately. It's not a big deal and I'll bring you back together immediately after we're done. Lucy, can you wait here with Officer Jones?"

"You mean I don't have to wait in jail?" Lucy asks.

"Of course not," Jessica says. "We will never put you in a jail cell."

"Ok, I'll wait here," Lucy says. "But only if you promise to cross your heart and hope to die and stick a needle in your eye, if you're lying."

Jessica laughs, and says, "I promise."

Lucy and I hug each other and I turn to follow Jessica, who ushers me into an empty room next door. She motions for me to sit at the table and pulls out a chair for me. She sits in a chair across from me.

"I know you're scared, but you don't need to be," she starts out.

Her voice is calm and smooth, maybe even a little comforting.

"I need you to tell me about you, your life and what you've been going through," she says, "so we can figure out the best way to take care of you and your sister. Let's start with your name."

"McCartney Matthews," I say, "but everybody calls me Cart. My daddy, who I know loves us and would be with us if he could, named me and my sister Lucy, after Paul McCartney and *Lucy in the Sky with Diamonds* from his favorite musical group, The Beatles."

"I like The Beatles, too," Jessica says. "*Yesterday* is one of my favorite songs."

She smiles warmly at me. Her friendly smile reminds me of my daddy's. It's a smile I haven't seen in a long time, except from Jack and Martha. Jessica's one act of kindness, a simple smile, is all it takes and I start the ugly, snot cry. I spill my guts from my earliest memories up until this very day, not leaving anything good, bad, or otherwise out. How pitiful is that? I must have rattled on for fifteen minutes. That makes twice now in a week. She looks up at me and then back down at her papers. Her poor hand seems like it can barely keep up with the notes she's taking.

When I finally stop, she asks if she can take some pictures of my injuries. I agree. I'll do anything to make Danny pay for what he's done. She hands me a box of tissues so I can wipe my face and blow my nose. She takes pictures of the side of my mouth and cheek, noting everything she sees, including the pinch mark on my arm. When I lift up my shirt part of the way, she snaps a photo of the bruises on my stomach where I was kicked.

"How much has Lucy seen throughout all of this?" she asks.

"I try to protect her from a lot of it," I say. "She wasn't home the day he attacked me in the dining room, but she was there this morning and saw him punch and kick me. It makes me sad that she's heard and seen far too much."

Jessica frowns as she writes a few more things down. She closes her notebook and thanks me for being so brave in talking to her and telling her all of this personal and painful stuff. She takes me back to Lucy, who runs to me, relieved Jessica held true to her promise.

"Are you ok?" Lucy asks. "Did she hurt you? I could hear you crying."

"I'm ok," I say. "It kind of felt good to get it all out, again. When she takes you next door, answer all of her questions honestly and don't leave anything out. And don't be scared. She's nice."

"Ok," Lucy says.

Jessica takes Lucy, and I sit in the room with Officer Jones. I don't feel much like talking, so I sit there staring at Jessica's certificate of diploma. It's in a black metal frame and hangs on the wall in front of me. The letters LCSW are behind her name. I don't know what those letters mean, but I hope they don't mean she can take Lucy away from me.

I think about everything in my life. I wonder where we'll go from here. Are they going to send us back with Mama and Danny? Will they believe them over us? Even after everything we've told them? Would Eleanor take us? If she did, would she help us find our daddy? Can I ask for Jack and Martha? I would like living with Jack and Martha and meeting their big family. I'd be able to find out what it is that makes everyone smile so big in all of their pictures.

But, what if they put us in foster care and separate us? I can't believe we've gone through all of this just to get separated. I can't live without Lucy. I won't live without her.

It doesn't take long for Lucy and Jessica to return. I scan Lucy's face for signs of trouble. She seems all right. Jessica leaves the room. Another officer comes in and brings us juice and crackers. Lucy and I don't realize how hungry we are until we polish everything off, even the seconds they bring us. It reminds me of yesterday morning at Jack and Martha's.

Shortly after, Mama, Eleanor and Jessica join us in the room. We move over to a table and chairs by the window. I look out at the dark clouds rolling in and hope it's not a sign of what's going to happen. Lucy and I sit on one side of the table, our chairs close together. Mama and Eleanor sit across from us, their chairs far apart. Jessica is on one end and Officer Jones is on the other end. Another officer I don't know is standing at the door.

No Danny. I wait for a minute, barely breathing, watching the door and half expecting an officer to usher him in. No one does. They did not bring Danny back here with us. I'm grateful, but I also wonder why not. Did they let him go free? Maybe they took him to get his car and he's coming back to take us home. Home. That's a joke. It's anything but a home. If that's the plan, going back *home*, then I'm making a different plan, like escaping and making a run for it as we exit the building. I wonder if we can out-run a cop. We're good at hiding. Maybe that would work better. Hide until the coast is clear. Jessica begins talking.

"I've had a chance to go over everyone's statements, as well as discuss the situation with the officers and detectives assigned to this case," she says, "and we've determined there is probable cause of domestic abuse, attempted sexual abuse and neglect of a minor on the part of Daniel Jackson and neglect of a minor on the part of June Thompson.

"What?" Mama stands up and yells. "What in the hell are you talking about? Danny has never laid a finger on those lying children."

"Ms. Thompson," Jessica says. "Please sit down."

"I will not sit down," Mama says. "This is bullshit. Danny never touched the little liar."

"Ms. Thompson," Jessica says. "The indentation on your daughter's face matches with the ring Mr. Jackson wears on his right hand. There is no denying it's a perfect match. It is proof that he struck your daughter in the face."

Mama stood there for a minute, dumbfounded and then, started in defending Danny. Even when presented with evidence, she still takes his side.

"I've done nothing but take care of these kids," Mama says. "I cook and clean and do their laundry. I do all of it."

"Ha," Lucy says. "You're the liar, Mama."

"I see you're developing your sister's smart mouth," Mama says. She turns to Jessica. "What have you done with Danny? Where is he?"

"Mr. Jackson will be remanded to jail until his court appearance."

"Jail?" Mama cries. She looks around the room at the officers, and finally at Eleanor.

"And that fat cow over there," she says, pointing, "has done nothing all of these years to help us out. It ain't easy raising two snot nosed kids with no support. Her no good son hasn't done shit."

"Officer Jones, please take Ms. Thompson away," Jessica instructs.

"You're finally going to get what you deserve," Eleanor yells after Mama.

"Mrs. Matthews," Jessica says, "I'm going to have to ask you to please refrain from making any remarks."

Eleanor sits quietly. But she looks pleased with herself.

"This brings us to the matter of temporary custody of the children," Jessica continues. "If we do not find suitable placement for them, they will go into the foster care system and there are no guarantees they will stay together. We need to determine what our options are and move forward quickly."

"No," Lucy and I scream.

We reach over and hug each other, sobbing.

"You promised," Lucy says to Jessica. "You lied."

"Lucy, I promised to bring you back to Cart, and I did," Jessica says. "If we can't find a family member or a close friend willing to take you both, I have no other choice. I am truly sorry."

Lucy sobs harder. I look over at Eleanor who is silent, looking down at her feet, and offering nothing.

37

"Nothing?" I scream, at the lady who is supposed to be my grandma. "After all we've been through you still can't step up and do the right thing?"

"I am in no position to take on two high spirited young girls," she says, not making eye contact with me, but instead with Jessica. "Jack has been a handful for me his entire life. I can't go through it all over again."

Jessica turns to one of the officers and instructs him to make a call to secure foster placement.

"No," I stand up and yell, banging my fist on the table. "I won't let you separate us. We'll run away again, if that's what it takes. No matter where you put us, or how many times you separate us, we will run away and find each other."

I look over at Eleanor and swear I see a tear forming in the corner of her eye. Could she have a heart in there after all?

"All we've ever wanted is to be loved, accepted and cared for, like a family is supposed to do," I say. "Our daddy is the only person who did. But it didn't take long for Mama and the war to screw that up for us. And Mama! She has been bringing loser boyfriends to her bed for years, but this is the first time one of them tried to get into ours. Do you know what it's like to live with that kind of fear? Having to place a chair under the door knob of your bedroom to make sure *he* doesn't sneak in at night and try to hurt you? Do you know what it feels like to have a smelly, beer soaked man reach up under your shirt and hear him say all of the awful things he wants to do to you? And if you don't let him, or try to tell anyone, he threatens to do the same thing to your baby sister, who you would die for, before letting him touch her? Do you *know* that feeling? It sucks. It totally sucks. Nobody deserves a life like that. Nobody."

That ugly, snot cry is taking over again. I'm losing control. I can't stop it. Lucy is crying and I sit back down and hug her, promising never to let go.

"Stop it," Eleanor yells.

She shakes her head and stands up and requests to speak to Jessica in the other room. They both leave. The officer who is left with us stands stoic at the door as Lucy and I sob. He walks over briefly, hands us a box of tissues, then returns to the door. He's standing guard, I guess. Maybe he thinks we'll try to escape. We will if they try to separate us. And if he steps out for even a second, Lucy and I are out of here.

After several minutes, Jessica and Eleanor return. I can see Eleanor has been crying. She dabs at her eyes with a handkerchief she has wadded up in her hand. And just like that, she turns and leaves the room with an officer. She doesn't look at us.

That's it? No goodbye? No, *I'm sorry. Have a great life. I hope things get better for you.* Nothing. Not a word, just tears and an exit. Well, thank you, Eleanor Matthews. Grandma. If I still had my Magic 8 Ball and could ask it if Eleanor was a horrible woman, I'm sure I'd peek inside and see, *Without A Doubt.*

Jessica sits down, takes a deep breath and looks at me and Lucy. I look away from her gaze, putting my head down, staring hard at Lucy's hand. I notice how soft and smooth her fingers are, intertwined with mine. Her knuckles are white, like mine.

I don't want to see Jessica's face, or anyone else's face when we're told we're being separated from each other and put into foster care. I look on the floor for our backpacks, and remember we don't have them. We left them in Eleanor's car when the police drove us here. We truly have nothing in this world.

I wonder if it's it too late to ask for Jack and Martha. Would they consider letting them raise us? Would Jack and Martha want us? They've shown us more love than any adult besides our daddy. Ever.

As Jessica begins to speak, I cry, which makes Lucy cry. I know what's coming. I can't stop it.

"Due to the pending charges against your mother and her boyfriend," Jessica begins, "and the fact that there is no suitable place for both of you to go, your grandmother has agreed to temporary custody, pending the court hearing, which will be in a month or so."

"What?" I say, not sure I heard her right. "Of us? Custody of us? Eleanor?"

"Does this mean we aren't going to be separated in foster care?" Lucy asks.

Jessica smiles her warm, friendly smile. "That's exactly what it means."

"If she's going to take us," Lucy asks, "why did she cry and leave?"

"Your grandmother seems like a tough lady," Jessica says, "But deep down she is kind-hearted. Don't forget that. She's been through rough things in her life, too. We could all learn to be more patient with each other."

"When is she coming back?" I ask.

"One of the officers took her back to her car," Jessica says. "She'll be back shortly with her car and your belongings."

Jessica leaves the room briefly and brings back sandwiches and cartons of milk for me and Lucy. We are eating the last of our food when Eleanor comes into the room. Her tears have long since dried and her features are once again hard and serious. She barely makes eye contact with me and Lucy. We're used to this kind of treatment, nothing new here. At least it's better than Mama and Danny or DCFS. Maybe we can still check into Jack and Martha. Eleanor looks as if she'd probably encourage it.

"I'll need you to sign a few things," Jessica says to Eleanor, who sits at the table.

Jessica points to the areas she wants Eleanor to sign, telling her it makes her responsible for us until the court hearing. Eleanor briefly looks up at me and Lucy. I look down in my lap, not wanting to see if she's going to change her mind and not sign. Apparently, she signs the papers. Jessica stands up, followed by Eleanor, and then they shake hands.

"We will be in touch, Mrs. Matthews," Jessica says. "I'll stop by your house in the morning to see how things are going."

"Very well, Ms. Barnes," Eleanor says.

She turns to look at me and Lucy.

"Are you girls ready?"

"Yes," I say hesitantly. Lucy and I stand and follow Eleanor out of the police station.

It's a quiet ride from the police station to Eleanor's house. As we pass through downtown, Eleanor seems distracted, like she's looking around for someone or something. There are a lot of people walking about, so maybe she's being extra careful not to hit any of them.

I see the restaurant across the plaza, where that horrible, homeless guy took our money and my Magic 8 Ball. I'd like to find him again. Give him a nice kick to the crotch to show my appreciation for taking the only money we had. We might never have been caught had it not been for him. We could have hidden out in a motel instead of the public park. But at least Danny's been caught and arrested. That's one good thing that cruddy homeless guy did for us, I guess. Soon, we pull up in Eleanor's driveway. She stops the car.

"Your bags are in the trunk," she says. "You can help me bring in your stuff."

We get out of the car and follow Eleanor around to the back. She unlocks the trunk with her key to reveal all of our stuff.

"Where did all of this come from?" I ask. "We only had two small backpacks."

"Yeah, well, I emptied your closet and dresser and brought your pillows," Eleanor says. "Your Mama and her boyfriend live like pigs."

"That's 'cause we aren't there to do the cleaning and cooking," Lucy says.

"Is that so?" Eleanor says.

"Mama couldn't clean her way out of a wet paper bag," Lucy says.

Eleanor and I both chuckle. Don't I know that's the truth. I don't know if it's a good thing or a bad thing Lucy's sounding more like me. I'd like to think when push comes to shove, she'll be able to take care of herself. I hope if I teach her anything, it's that.

We carry all of our belongings into Eleanor's house. She leads us down the hallway to a room. She opens the door and turns on the light. Lucy and I step inside. The walls are yellow. Lucy looks over at me and I don't say a word.

"I'll let you two get settled," Eleanor says, leaving the bags she carried with us. "The bathroom is across the hall if you need it. Go ahead and get unpacked. You can use the two dressers here and there are hangers in the closet."

Eleanor turns and closes the door behind her. Lucy and I throw our pillows at the head of bed. We lie down and check out the surroundings. The bed sits in the middle of the room, facing the door. The walls are yellow, but it's a light yellow and looks fairly tolerable with all of the white things in the room.

I especially love the white chenille bedspread with the rose patterns and ball tassels. The throw rugs near the bed and the curtains on the window all match with the bedspread. Sunlight fills the room. I can see out the window into a park-like backyard. Looking back inside, there are white framed pictures of flowers on the walls, as well as a crucifix near the door.

It feels safe here. I feel like I can let my guard down a little. Lucy must feel it too. She snuggles in next to me. We fall into a deep sleep.

38

"Cart," Lucy says, shaking me awake. "I think we've been sleeping a long time."

I open my eyes and look around, confused for a minute. Then, it registers where we are. I look out the window. The sun is no longer streaming in the window.

"I guess we have been," I say. "We better get our things put away."

We stumble out of bed and start unpacking. It's strange we each have our own dresser. And the bed is twice the size of the bed we shared at Danny's. We hang a few things in the closet and open the door and walk down the hallway to find Eleanor. She is in the kitchen cooking. It smells delicious. I notice some cookies and milk at the table.

"I thought I heard you moving around," Eleanor says. "There's a snack on the table to hold you over until dinner is ready. I'm making Sloppy Joes. I hope you both like them."

"Sure," we say.

We sit down at the table and each eat a chocolate chip cookie.

"I guess we fell asleep," I say, after taking a bite, and a sip of milk.

"I know," Eleanor says. "I peeked in on you to make sure you were ok."

I'm not sure what to say. No one has ever made sure we were ok. Except for Daddy, but that's been so long ago. Eleanor still seems a bit distant and cold, but somehow softer. I can't explain it.

"Is that ok?" I ask. "Should we have been helping you?"

"If you're tired you should sleep," Eleanor says. "I would imagine you didn't sleep well the night before outside, wherever that was."

Lucy and I don't tell her we slept in her other car, or someone's car, in the garage on the other side of the house. That can probably wait for another day.

"Dinner will be ready in about an hour," she says. "If you have unpacking to do, you could finish it up now."

Lucy and I admit we still have some to do, so we head back to our room. Lucy goes into the bedroom and I stop at the bathroom. Closing the door behind me, I feel the need to cry. I try to keep it quiet. I'm not sure why I'm crying. Maybe it's relief. Maybe this time things will go right.

I wipe my face and eyes off with a piece of toilet paper and blow my nose. I look at my reflection in the mirror. I wish I looked more like my daddy. Like Lucy does. This copper hair of mine makes me a dead ringer for Mama. But my blue eyes are Daddy's. I'm glad for that. I gaze into my own eyes and pretend it's Daddy gazing back at me. It feels nice.

I reach in my pocket for a hair band, then finger brush and smooth out my wild locks and wrap it in a ponytail. I wonder if Eleanor would let me dye my hair. Any color other than Mama's would be fine with me. I join Lucy in the bedroom. We both work silently, putting our clothes away. We're almost finished, when I hear Lucy clear her throat.

"I heard you crying," she says, putting her clothes in the dresser, making sure not to look at me. "Are you ok?"

"Don't you have elephant ears?" I say, with half a smile. "I hope everything is finally going to be ok. It feels like maybe it could be. I don't know what else to do or where to turn if it fails this time."

"Dinner is ready," Eleanor calls out.

She doesn't have to tell me and Lucy twice. We waste no time getting to the table. As we eat, I ask Eleanor what the other rooms are behind the closed doors in the hallway. I don't want to make Eleanor mad and have her send us away, but I'm curious if one of those rooms is Daddy's and if any of his stuff is still inside it.

"The first room on the left is my room," she says. "Then it's the bathroom and yours and Lucy's room across from that and the room at the end of the hall is Jack's."

My ears perk up. Eleanor becomes silent for a moment, hesitating on what she's going to say next. She looks up at me and Lucy. I'm sure she notices my eyes, wide and anxious.

"I'll show you Jack's room after dinner and dishes," she says somewhat reluctantly.

I smile the biggest smile I can remember. It feels strange to my face. Even Lucy notices and smiles too.

"That would make me the happiest ever," I say.

I reach up to wipe away a tear. You'd think I'd be all out of tears by this time.

I speed through dinner and help Eleanor with the dishes. It's time. I feel like a kid going into a candy store as we head down the hall to Daddy's room. Finally, something that can make him feel close to me again. At least, I hope so. My eyes tear up thinking about it. I'm not sure when I turned into such a baby.

I find it almost impossible to breathe as Eleanor opens the door to his bedroom and reaches inside to flip on the light switch. I never in my wildest dreams ever thought I'd have a chance to see anything of Daddy's again.

I'm not sure what to take in first as we step inside the room behind Eleanor.

"You might want to breathe," Lucy says, nudging me from behind.

Pushing out a deep breath, I gaze at Daddy's bed which is covered in a blue spread with matching curtains on the two windows. I walk over and rub the bedspread with my hand, then sit on the bed. I grab his pillow and squeeze it, pretending it's him. I hold the pillow up to my nose and take in a deep sniff, hoping to smell a trace of him or his Brut cologne. I swear I can but it may be my imagination. I hug his pillow again and close my eyes. I'm sure Eleanor and Lucy think I'm weird, but I need that hug right now more than anything.

"Daddy always said Brut was a chick magnet," I say, half-muffled in the pillow.

A feeling of euphoria has come over me.

"I never knew what he meant," I say, "but I laughed with him when he laughed because his laugh just made me want to laugh, too."

I'm sure I'm rambling and not making much sense to them. How many times can you say laugh in a sentence without being told you're weird? Eleanor looks away and Lucy looks at me like I've completely gone insane. She doesn't remember anything about Daddy. That makes me sad. There is so much of him worth remembering.

I see a wooden desk in the corner with a chair tucked into it. Did he sit there to do his homework? Or maybe daydream about what his future would be like? It's then I gasp when I notice the Beatles bobblehead collection lined up across the length of the desk. I nearly faint. I was afraid that I had somehow dreamed them up and they weren't real.

"The bobbleheads!" I cry out, setting the pillow down and moving over to them. "I haven't seen them since I was little and Daddy played Beatles music on the record player. He used to set the bobbleheads in motion and we all danced together."

"Your daddy had them sent here along with some of his other things when June kicked him out."

I barely hear Eleanor as I touch each bobblehead with love. I can't stop the tears from falling down my cheeks. It is such an overwhelming feeling to see them again. I notice each one has been dusted. In fact, everything in this room is dust-free. Clearly, Eleanor comes in here and dusts regularly. Does that mean she misses him and loves him? Or maybe that he comes home?

"Did Daddy send his record player and records here too?" I ask.

"Yes, they're in the closet." She points toward it.

"Can I listen to them?"

"Yes," Eleanor says. She turns to Lucy.

"Let's give Cart a moment alone. Maybe you'd like a warm bubble bath. I'll help you get it started."

Lucy agrees and they both leave the room. I walk over to the closet door and open it. The smell of Brut greets me. I smile. Some of Daddy's shirts are hanging up in the closet. Does he still come here? Could it be possible? Is Eleanor holding out on us?

I cover myself in his shirts, inhaling the smell of Brut so deeply, it hurts my chest. I take one of the shirts off the hanger and put it on. It's blue and green flannel. I feel like I'm wrapped in a hug. I roll up the sleeves and reach down to the floor for the box of records. Pulling it out of the closet, I see that it's most of his Beatles collection. I push the box over to the desk, and look for the record player. I find it hidden toward the back of the closet. It's heavy. Eleanor comes back into the room and helps me. She takes it and places it on the desk.

"Can I ask you something?" I say to her.

"Yes," she says, hesitating.

She seems like she doesn't want to answer questions, especially from me. I sit on the bed and she sits on the chair by the desk and looks at me. I can hear Lucy in the bathroom singing as the water fills up the tub.

"What made you change your mind?" I ask. "About taking us, I mean, even if it's just for a little while."

Eleanor sighs. It's a deep, heavy sigh. A sigh that says there is a sad story to go with it. I can see by the look on her face she's not quite sure what she wants to say. She must have decided not to hold anything back, as what she said next I wouldn't have seen coming in a million years.

39

"When I was eighteen years old," Eleanor begins, "I left home, to see the world. I didn't want to get stuck in Small Town, Nowhere. I knew I was meant for more than what I could achieve here. My parents objected, but I was stubborn and thought I knew everything. So, I packed up my car and hit the road."

"What were you going to do?" I ask.

"Go to California and live with my cousin," she says. "The people in the movie industry were looking for extras. My cousin said she made decent money doing it. I was star struck, so I agreed to go."

"That seems pretty brave," I say.

"Hindsight will tell you it was extremely stupid."

I don't say anything as I watch Eleanor's face. It turns from a reminiscing look to that of fear, panic, and then, anger. It reminds me of me when I think about Danny. I wait for her to continue.

"On the way out there, my car broke down," she says. "The town it happened in was small. I'm not even sure what the name of it was. Lucky for me, it had a repair garage. Or so I thought it was lucky. I walk into the office door of the garage to find a grubby, old man sitting behind the desk. His clothes were dirty and his teeth were either missing or blackened. He spit chewing tobacco into a cup. He was disgusting but I thought as long as he could fix my car, that's all that mattered."

Eleanor pauses and takes a deep breath. She doesn't look at me.

"The old man made the hair on my arms stand up. I wasn't sure why. Maybe it was his gruff manner, or the way his blue eyes seemed to pierce right through me, as he eyed me up and down. I wanted to leave, but didn't have a working car, so didn't have much of a choice. A young guy, probably close to my age, cowered in a corner, not making eye contact with me or the old guy. After I told the old guy what happened to my car, he sent the young guy to get it with the tow truck. I told him I didn't have much money but I'd pay him what I could. He smiled a black, toothless smile and said we'd work it out. The boy returned and backed my car into the shop with his truck. The old man told him to go home. He said to tell his wife he'd be late and to keep his dinner warm. The young guy must have been his son. He told him he was going to stay and fix my car so I could get back on the road. It was already getting dark at this point. The old man said there was a room off the shop area where I could wait. It had a pop machine if I was thirsty."

I watch Eleanor's face. Tears flow gently down her cheeks. She hesitates, but continues forward.

"I followed him from the office into the shop, where I saw my car. He opened the door to the room and motioned for me to go in first. I hesitated. It was dark and scary, but finally, I stepped inside. The old man followed me in, locking the door behind him. I stood there in the dark, not sure what to do. I asked him if he was going to turn on a light. He didn't answer. My heartbeat grew faster as panic rose from my chest to my throat. I felt like screaming, but nothing would come out. The old man brushed past me. I should have felt for the door and ran like hell. My feet wouldn't budge. He turned on a small lamp, barely lighting the room. I looked around for the pop machine and a chair to sit on, or maybe a coffee table with magazines. There was none of that. There was a table with the lamp and a bed. I cried out and dashed for the door. He caught and stopped me."

Tears fill my eyes and my heart feels heavy. I know what Eleanor is going to say next. I peek up at her face, contorted with pain. My heart is breaking for her. I feel sick to my stomach.

"He raped me," she says softly, looking down at her feet. "He said a young thing like me, out in the world on her own, needs to see that it is a big and dangerous place and maybe I should go back home where it's safe. He laughed like he was the devil himself, as he got up off of me and pulled up his pants."

Tears stream down my face as I listen.

"He said if I told anyone what happened, he'd call the police and tell them I tried to run out of here without paying. He said I was a stranger in town and he had lived there all of his life. People knew him and trusted him. No one would believe me. I was young and stupid and believed him. He fixed my car as I sat on the bed crying."

Eleanor pulls a handkerchief from her pocket, dabs her eyes and blows her nose.

"He finally unlocked the door and let me out when my car was done. He didn't charge me for the repair, saying it was a sweet trade and that I could come back and get my car repaired anytime. He slapped me hard on the butt as I walked past him to my car. I had never been with a guy before. California didn't look appealing anymore, so I went back home. Nine months later, your daddy was born. I had shamed my parents. Only bad girls had a child out of wedlock. I told them what happened, thinking they'd feel bad for me and not blame me, but they didn't believe me. They thought I was lying to hide the fact that I was a tramp. I was devastated. I wasn't a tramp. I had been a virgin. Jack was so tiny and fragile. My parents made me keep him as punishment for my bad behavior. I loved and despised him at the same time. He looked a lot like that old man and his son, but I saw myself in him, too. Raising someone and loving them under conditions like that isn't easy. When he got bigger, he would ask me about his daddy and finally, I told him he died in a war. He was too young to understand the truth. I couldn't bring myself to tell him what really happened, even once he was grown. I almost started believing my own lies."

"You mean, Daddy never knew?" I ask. "He used to tell me he thought you hated him because you never showed him any love."

"I tried to love him," she says. "I really did. He looked so much like that man and his son. Like Lucy. She has similar features. And your eyes are a dead ringer for his, theirs. That's how I knew you were both Jack's. I wanted to run from both of you. I didn't need two more faces reminding me of a past I never asked for. But when you told me what that scum Danny was pulling with you, I couldn't let you go back there. I just couldn't. I know the pain, fear and anger far too well. I couldn't let you go through that. It's time to break the cycle."

I feel like I need to hug Eleanor. Would she let me? Would she get mad? I hug her anyway and whisper I'm sorry and thank you into her ear. She hugs me back. We linger in the hug an extra minute. It feels good. I can hear Lucy singing in the tub. I'm not sure how much I should tell her. She doesn't miss anything. I'm sure she heard us talking. I don't have time, nor do I want to focus on the fact that I'm here because my grandmother was raped. That's heavy stuff. I have other pressing things on my mind, like my daddy. I pull back from Eleanor.

"I have to ask," I say. "Is my daddy still alive?"

Eleanor looks at me. It's a look I've seen before from her. It's a *'how do I tell you this'* look. I don't want to hear he's dead. Immediately, I'm sorry I asked. Maybe there is something to the saying *ignorance is bliss*. Before she can answer, the phone rings.

"I have to answer it," she says. "It could be important."

She leaves me standing there, on the edge of a cliff, hanging. Is he dead? Is he alive? He has to be dead. What other reason would he have for not trying to find me and Lucy? I hear the tub water draining. Before long, Lucy comes in, all clean, shiny and smiling.

"You look awful," she says. "What's going on?"

"Eleanor just gave me some history, that's all," I say. "I'll tell you some of it later."

"Ok. Where'd she go?" Lucy asks.

"She's on the phone," I say.

We couldn't make out what she was saying, but heard her say thank you and hang up. She came back into Daddy's room, her face sadder than when she left.

"We need to go to the hospital," she says.

"Hospital?" I ask. "Who's at the hospital?"

"Jack."

"Daddy?" I cry. "He's alive? I was sure you were going to tell me before the phone rang that he's dead. I can't believe it."

I hug Lucy and jump up and down.

"Before you get too excited," Eleanor says, "I need to tell you, Jack is very sick. He has a severe alcohol and drug addiction and is not himself anymore. He hasn't been for a long time. I didn't want you to know or see him like that. I didn't want to tarnish your wonderful memory of him with the knowledge of how he is now. They're not sure he's going to survive this time. I think you should go with me to see him and to tell him goodbye."

"Goodbye? No," I cry. "We just found him. I don't want to tell him goodbye. He can't die. He just can't die."

40

It doesn't take long to get to the hospital. So many things are running through my head. Will Daddy recognize me and Lucy? Will we recognize him? I know years of drug and alcohol abuse can change a person, but once he sees us, will it jar a memory? Can we bring him back from the edge and nurse him back to health? He has to live. Please, God, let him live.

"Are you ok, Cart?" Lucy asks.

I look down at my hands and see they are visibly shaking. I can't speak. It's all so overwhelming. Lucy grabs my hand as the three of us walk into the hospital emergency room.

Daddy has been taken upstairs already. Eleanor's shoes click down the sterile, white hallway toward the elevator. Her steps echo for miles. We find the elevator and push the button for the second floor. Stepping off the elevator, Eleanor heads towards the nurse's station, with us closely in tow behind her.

"I'm sorry, Ma'am," a nurse says, "but the children aren't allowed up here."

"That's rubbish," Eleanor says. "We are here to see their father, who may or may not live. They haven't seen him in a very long time and no one is going to prevent them from seeing him now."

The nurse purses her lips and narrows her eyes, looking Eleanor up and down. Eleanor crosses her arms as she taps her foot. It's a stance I'm becoming quite familiar with. Inwardly, I chuckle. It usually means she's going to get her way.

"What's the room number for Jack Matthews?" she asks.

"Very well, then," the nurse responds, fanning through the sheets on her clipboard. "He's in room 235. Make it a short visit."

"We will take all of the time the girls need," Eleanor says.

With that, Eleanor carries on down the hall. We look over at the nurse, who glares back at us. We hurry to catch up with Eleanor before the nurse changes her mind. We see her turn into a room at the end of the hall.

By the time we catch up to her, she's already at his bedside. Lucy and I stand in the doorway for a minute. I'm scared to go in. It wouldn't look good if I vomited in the hallway, but I feel like I'm going to anyway. Lucy squeezes my hand and looks over at me. Another nurse moves us to the side as she enters the room.

"I have your son's belongings, Mrs. Matthews," the nurse says.

She's carrying a dirty duffle bag that must belong to Daddy. In her other hand is my macramé bag. My bag? What the hell? Why does she have my bag? It was stolen. I let go of Lucy's hand and push the nurse and Eleanor to the side, stealing a long look at the man in the bed. Daddy. His beard is overgrown and matted, as well as the hair on his head. His cheeks are rough and reddened, aged. So aged. He no longer smells of Brut. He is no longer a chick magnet. My long-lost daddy, who I love more than anything on this earth, is the man who stole my bag, my money and my Magic 8 Ball.

I don't know what to say. I run back to Lucy and hug her and cry. All I can do is cry.

"Cart?" Lucy asks, confused. "Is he dead? Why are you crying?"

"He's the guy from the restaurant who stole our stuff," I say.

"Do we have the wrong room?" Lucy asks.

"No, we have the right room," Eleanor says. "Please girls, come in. Cart, I told you your daddy is not what he used to be."

I point to the macramé bag in the nurse's hand.

"That's my bag," I say. "Daddy stole it when we were in the restaurant. It had all of our money in it, my Magic 8 Ball, a picture, a card, and a penlight we took from Danny."

The nurse opens up the bag and looks inside.

"Everything you said except the money," she says.

"Not surprising," Eleanor says.

"This can't be real," I say.

The nurse closes the bag and hands it to me.

"Come here, Cart," Eleanor commands.

For once, I do what I'm told. I move to stand next to Eleanor, who is standing next to Daddy. Lucy follows closely behind me.

"I feel like I'm mostly to blame for the way your daddy is," she says, stroking his matted, filthy hair. "Nurse, please have someone shave his beard and hair off immediately and clean him up. We are going to get a soda and be back shortly."

"Yes, Ma'am," the nurse replies.

There's something about Eleanor that commands attention. When she calls an order, people seem to listen. It's intimidating and empowering at the same time.

We leave the room and head to the cafeteria. As we sit at a table sipping a soda, Eleanor talks, so we listen.

"I should have showed your daddy more love," she begins, staring into the Styrofoam cup. "It wasn't his fault how things were. He never knew that though. He kept searching for love. I knew that, but I was so damn stubborn.

He thought he found that love in June, but she was incapable of love, as I'm sure you've both figured out. But he knew he found the love he was missing when you girls were born. I know he adored you, but the war messed him up, and he got into drugs while over there. By the time he came back, he was too far gone, so your mama gave him the boot. He did try to find you, but your mama kept moving you. Finally, the will for drugs took over his will to find you. It wasn't your fault. It wasn't his fault. Drugs and alcohol are powerful and overwhelming destroyers. You don't know you've been destroyed until it's too late. That's what happened to your daddy."

I hate the man lying upstairs in that hospital bed. Why did he have to be so damn weak? For a man who has searched his whole life for love, he sure dropped the ball when he finally found it. I would have done anything for him. I think I would still do anything for him. That's what makes it hurt so much.

"How can someone say they love you," I say, "and then be so quick to throw it all away? I want my daddy back."

"We can bring him back," Lucy says. "If he survives this hospital stay, we'll bring him home and love him and take care of him."

"If anyone could bring him back," Eleanor says, "it would be the two of you."

"I don't want him to die," I say. "If he survives this time, we will do whatever it takes."

Lucy, Eleanor and I go back to Daddy's room. The nurses have him cleaned up. Looking at him, I feel overwhelmed at once. He looks more like my daddy, just older. He's still not awake. I want to crawl up next to him and nuzzle into him, but don't. I wouldn't want him to wake up and freak out. The doctor enters the room and looks at Lucy and I, then Eleanor.

"We've run some preliminary tests," he begins, "and we think he's going to pull through. He's incredibly fortunate. I'm not sure how much more his body can take. I don't know how much his memory will have suffered due to the drugs and alcohol. It's going to be a long recovery, but if he has support and stays away from substances and gets into rehab, he stands a chance."

Eleanor sighs. The look of relief on her face is obvious.

"When can we bring him home?" I ask.

"He'll be here a few days at least," the doctor says. "He'll need meds to control the cravings. He may be difficult and have anger flare ups and he'll need to get counseling. I don't know how much his memory has been affected. He may not remember any of you for a short time, a long time, or ever."

Ever. The word gives me goose bumps. How cruel is it to find your daddy only to have him not know who you are. *Ever.*

"We won't *ever* give up on him," I say.

Eleanor, Lucy and I leave the hospital. We're going home to get the house ready for daddy. I pray it's a new beginning and not a final ending. As I sit in the back seat of Eleanor's car, I slide out my Magic 8 Ball. I don't want Eleanor to notice from the front seat. I close my eyes and shake it. "Will my daddy *ever* remember us and love us again?"

Reply Hazy, Try Again.

Every time I ask the Magic 8 Ball a question about my daddy, this is the answer it gives me. Every time.

222

41

It takes Daddy five days in the hospital to be stable enough to leave. He's been home for two weeks and still nothing. He doesn't know or recognize any of us. I look into his eyes and they are expressionless, almost dead. It makes me sad. They don't have the sparkle they used to have. When I was little and looked into my daddy's eyes I could see passion and excitement straight from his soul, shining back at me.

Nothing shines back at me now. It's hard not to give up hope. Daddy doesn't talk much either, a grunt here and there. Eleanor says it could be the meds. I'm afraid it could be something else, like he fried his brains forever. Feeling sorry for myself, I barely hear the doorbell ring. I see Eleanor walk to the door and open it. I peek over.

"Jack and Martha," I yell, running to the door.

Eleanor steps to the side as I hug Martha and then Jack. Despite everything that has happened, it's so good to see them again.

"Come in," Eleanor says. "You must know Cart."

"Oh, we don't want to be a bother," Martha says. "Our friend on the police force told us the girls are staying here."

"We just stopped to say hi," Jack adds. "Are you girls doing ok? I feel bad the way things were left. We've been thinking about you and praying for you every day."

"Come in and I'll get some lemonade," Eleanor says. "You can catch up with the girls."

Lucy enters the room as Jack and Martha take a seat at the dining room table. She looks at me to make sure it's ok, and runs over to hug them both. She's happy to see them.

"You make the best bacon ever," Lucy says, sniffing Martha for signs of bacon.

Martha chuckles.

"You are the best bacon eater ever," she says. "I don't know where you put it all. You must have yourself a hollow leg."

Eleanor brings lemonade and joins us at the table.

"So, how is it you know the girls?" she asks.

"They came to us a while back, thinking maybe I was their daddy," Jack says, with a chuckle.

Eleanor raises an eyebrow at Jack. Jack's deep laughter fills the room.

"It's not how it sounds," he says. "My name is Jack Matthews, just like their daddy's. The girls found my name and number in the phone book and were hoping I was their long lost daddy. Apparently, that was not the case."

"So it would seem," Eleanor says with a laugh.

"The good Lord knows we felt horrible," Martha continues. "After the girls explained their situation to us, we felt helpless and confided in our friend on the force."

"He had no choice but to report it," Jack adds. "Had I known that, I wouldn't have said a single word to him. It broke our hearts the day they ran off. We tried to find them. We drove all over Freeport. They did not want to be found."

"Except that horrible Danny found us anyway," Lucy says. "He's in jail now. I hope they throw away the key and he never gets out."

"You and me too, honey," Martha says. "Did you find your daddy?"

There's an uncomfortable silence. Eleanor excuses herself, saying she needs to get something out of the oven.

"I'm sorry, it's none of my business," Martha adds. "Looks like you found your grandma and you both look well and happy and that's all that matters."

"Daddy's here," I say. "He's lying down right now."

"That's a wonderful thing then," Jack adds.

"Not really," Lucy says. "He's our daddy, but not really our daddy."

"Child, what are you saying?" Martha asks.

"Daddy has an addiction to drugs and alcohol and he doesn't remember anything," I say. "I don't know if he ever will."

"I see," Jack says. "I will pray for him."

"Do you remember the things you used to do with your daddy?" Martha asks.

"Yes," I say. "All of it, the music, the lightning bugs, dancing and laughing. And love. Real love. Daddy truly did love us."

"Show him all of that love," she says, "Maybe it will spark a memory."

"I know, we've been trying for weeks, but it's hard. It's like he's not really our Daddy," I say.

"He's in there," Martha says, pointing to my heart, then stands. "Don't lose the faith. You need to keep believing that. We should be on our way."

"We are so happy you are well," Jack says, standing. "Please stop by and see us any time."

"I'll make sure I have bacon on hand at all times," Martha says to Lucy.

"Oh, we will be stopping by," Lucy says.

We walk Jack and Martha to the door. I'm happy they stopped.

After Jack and Martha leave, I think about what she said. Maybe it's time we bring daddy back to us by making him remember all of the good things we did together. That night after dinner, Lucy helps me bring out the record player and a Beatles album.

"Daddy," I say, grabbing his hands, "stand up. It's time to dance. You remember how we used to dance when I was little, don't you?"

Daddy stands but doesn't answer. I plug the record player cord into the wall, and place the album on the turntable. I lift the needle and place it on the record. *Help!* comes blasting out and I hold Daddy's hand as I dance around him.

"Remember this song, Daddy?" I say. "It's one of your favorites. It's the Beatles. I know you remember the Beatles. You could never forget them."

I look at Daddy. Nothing. His eyes are still blank. I dance to every song on that album until we get to the song, *Yesterday,* near the end of the record. I listen to the words. I squeeze my daddy and cry into his shirt. I can't give up on him.

~

Every morning, I wake up Daddy and splash Brut cologne on his cheeks, telling him the chicks are waiting for him. Every night, Daddy and I dance to the Beatles music. We get out the bobbleheads and he watches them bobble. Lucy looks at his face to see if he recognizes any of the songs. It's the same blank stare, song after song, night after night. It's getting harder to keep this up.

"Hey, Cart," Lucy says. "Tonight let's go outside and catch lightning bugs with Daddy."

"It's not going to do any good," I say, feeling down and broken.

"You are not giving up," Lucy says. "Our daddy is worth it and you know it. Maybe tonight will be the night."

226

"I'm not giving up," I say. "It's hard to see him like this. I'd give anything to see that spark in his eyes."

"Daddy loves us," Lucy says. "And if the old daddy never comes back, at least we have this daddy and that's better than no daddy."

Lucy's right, kind of. But she never knew the old daddy, or at least can't remember him. I do though. I long for that daddy so bad it hurts my heart. How many nights in a row can someone cry and hope and dream and pray before giving up?

I sit next to Daddy on the patio chair as Lucy runs around catching lightning bugs. I help her put them into an old peanut butter jar, just like we did when we were little. I hold the jar up to Daddy. He holds his finger up and traces over the jar where the sparkly bugs light up. At the end of the night we release them, just like we did back then.

"It's time to let them go, Daddy," I say. "No one wants to die in captivity, remember?"

Daddy watches as I open the jar lid and shake the bugs out. Stunned for a moment, they soon light up and fly away into the night. Just like my daddy's memories.

42

This morning, Eleanor and I are going to the courthouse. Lucy is staying home to keep an eye on Daddy. I am nervous about seeing Danny again. Eleanor says I have nothing to worry about. If he is dumb enough to do something stupid, she'll be right there to stop him dead in his tracks. *And I mean dead* she says with a menacing grin. Danny would be a fool to mess with Eleanor.

I get goose bumps when Danny enters the court room. His lawyer has him dressed in a suit and tie. It still doesn't conceal the creep that he is. He looks over at me and smiles one of his sickening smiles. Eleanor leans in front of me and shoots Danny a deadly glare, daring him to try something. It doesn't take the judge long to hear the case and sentence Danny. He's getting three years in prison, minus time served. It isn't long enough for me, but it's better than nothing. At least, I don't have to look over my shoulder for another three years. Mama is there. She cries when he is sentenced. She hasn't tried to get a hold of us or come see us at all. I wonder who is taking care of her. Mama doesn't like to be alone. I wouldn't be surprised if she already has some unknowing, boyfriend on the side.

The judge raps his gavel and court is dismissed. They lead Danny out of the room. I can't look at him. Mama looks at Eleanor and me, but she doesn't come over. She doesn't say hi, how's it going, are you ok? Nothing. Mama is for sure a crappy mama but it still hurts to see her act like this. I don't ever want to have to live with her again, but it'd be nice to know that somewhere in there she truly does love us. I guess I won't hold my breath for that day.

Eleanor signs the papers to have indefinite custody of me and Lucy. I should probably start calling her grandma. She has definitely earned the title. We stop at the bakery and bring home cookies to celebrate.

"Lucy," I call. "We're home."

She doesn't answer. I don't hear music playing. The house is eerily quiet. What if Daddy had a bad spell and wigged out on Lucy? We didn't think about that when we left her here with him this morning.

"Eleanor, I don't know where they are," I say, panic rising.

"I'll go look in the bedrooms and downstairs," she says. "You look out back."

Eleanor takes off in the direction of the bedrooms and I head for the back door. I open it and stand on the stoop to yell, then stop. Lucy is sitting in a patio chair, her back to me, holding Daddy's hands while talking to him. He's staring off into space, but that doesn't stop her.

"Listen Daddy," I hear her say, shaking his hands in hers, willing him to pay attention. "I know you're inside there somewhere. You need to come out of there and act like our daddy again. Do you hear me? We all need you, but Cart especially needs you. I may not remember anything about you, but Cart remembers everything. Please don't let Cart down, Daddy. I'm going to be honest, you let her down once and I'm not going to stand here and watch you let her down again. Come back to us and then keep yourself straightened up."

229

Lucy lets go of Daddy's hands and gently shakes his shoulders. Tears bite at my eyes. Lucy. No matter what happens, she has my back. I take a deep breath.

"There you are," I say, "I've been looking for you."

"Daddy and I are out here getting some fresh air and talking," she says. "Well, I'm doing all of the talking and I'm not so sure he's listening. But he better be."

"I'm sure in his own way he's listening," I say. "And thank you. Thank you for always having my back. I love you more than anything, Lucy."

Lucy stands and I walk to her. We embrace. It's almost like we're transferring our energy to one another. I know no matter what happens, as long as I have Lucy, I will have the energy to face another day.

That night after dinner, Eleanor sits in her chair reading the paper and Lucy is reading her book. I pull out the bobbleheads and set them on the table next to Daddy. I put an album on the turntable and move the needle over to the record. *Twist and Shout* begins to play, just like it did that day so long ago. I set each one of the heads bobbing to the music.

"Look, Daddy," I say. "The bobbleheads are dancing. Do you remember them?"

Daddy watches the heads bob. I bobble my head too and giggle, just like I did when I was little. As I sit next to him, as close as I can get, I sniff him. I can't help it. I've always had to sniff him. He still smells like my daddy, even if he can't act like it. I nuzzle into him, close my eyes and pretend it's oh so many years ago, and I'm little again. I dream Daddy is laughing and dancing with me as I sniff him. He catches me smelling him again.

"Brut's a chick magnet, Cart," Daddy says, quietly, hoarsely.

I jerk my eyes open and turn to him.

"Did you say that or did I dream it?"

I look into Daddy's eyes. I see a tiny bit of spark as a slight smile crosses his lips.

"Can't keep 'em off me with this stuff on."

I laugh and cry and hug my daddy. And for the first time in a long time, I feel him hugging me back.

~

That night, I sneak out of bed, open my macramé bag and pull the Magic 8 Ball out. I haven't touched it since the day we found Daddy. I have been too afraid. I take a deep breath, and shake that ball as hard as I can, and whisper, "Is my daddy going to be ok?"

As I See It, Yes.

Special Thanks...

Thank you to my family and friends, especially my parents, my husband Ken, and my children Ashley, Anthony and Anna, for your endless support. I'm not sure you completely understood my crazy obsession, but maybe now that the book is here, you will.

Thank you to my beautiful grandchildren for being my spark and my joy. I love you more than anything.

An extra special thank you to my niece, Emma, and her cousin, Reese, for being my cover models. I appreciate you weathering the rain and mosquitos in order to get the perfect shot.

Thank you Ash Ahrens for taking the perfect shot!

A super special thank you to Emma, Lynn, Amy, Mary, and Kathleen, for being my faithful beta readers throughout this process. Your insight, honesty and feedback made this a much better book.

Thank you to my social media guru, Mike, for helping me curb my willy nilly tendencies. I'm sure I was a challenge.

Thank you to those who purchased my book. I hope you laughed, cried, and got angry at the situations in which my characters found themselves. If so, my work here is done!

About The Author

Debbie Winnekins Deutsch was born and raised in Northwest Illinois. She was one of those kids who'd sneak a stack of books and a flashlight under the covers and read until she fell asleep or got caught. As she grew, so did her love for books and eventually writing. Throw Away Sisters is her first YA novel. She has a husband, grown children, beautiful grandchildren, and two cats and a dog who think they are in charge. Debbie's Motto: Don't be afraid to express yourself. Write. Draw. Paint. Sing. Dance. Do it for you. Believe in you. Have fun. Find that spark and you'll always have joy in your heart.